Felix O'Neill and his friend Dr. Garzon investigate the secret sciences of the shapeshifter, the berserker and the werewolf. Here the master detective tries to solve a mystery in a remote swampland where a cunning murderer has terrorized the simple folk of the old waterways, jungles and fens.

LIFE OF DREW CARSON

Sam Drew Carson was born in the North of Ireland and educated there at Wellington College and the Ulster Polytechnic. He completed his education in the USA at New Mexico Highlands University and the University of Arkansas and has traveled widely in North America, around the Atlantic and in Europe.

Drew worked as a seaman and fish-gutter in Vestmannaeyjar off the coast of Iceland. He lived and worked in the Irish and Western Isles Gaeltachts and was married in Welsh-speaking Carmarthen after which he honeymooned in Belfast.

He has told his stories, composed and sung his songs, seeking storylines in Bristol and the English Westcountry. Drew has also lived and written in Nashville, Tennessee, in the wooded hills of Mid-America and from the Appalachians to the Ozarks. This was the culture that gave rise to the now worldwide Scotch-Irish country music.

In the USA, he also worked beside the bayous of the French-speaking Cajuns in the South and among the Western Spanish-speaking Navajos, Apaches and Pueblos of the Sangre de Cristo Mountains in New Mexico.

Drew has sailed far into the seas of old Gaelic and Oriental legend. After many years searching for inspiration for story and music, the author is still traveling and writing.

BOOKS BY DREW CARSON

SAGA OF TSUNAMI –
the Trilogy, 2nd edition
ISBN: 978-0-9561435-1-8

ZENISUB –
Fun and Games in Businezz
ISBN: 978-0-9561435-2-5

GOOD FOR A LAUGH –
Six Funny Playscripts for Amateurs
ISBN: 978-0-9561435-3-2

HOME WITH A GOOD COMPANION –
Amateur Pantomime Scripts for a Merry Winter
ISBN: 978-0-9561435-4-9

BACK TO THE GOOD OLD DAYS –
Miracle Plays of Sunlight and Shadow
ISBN: 978-0-9561435-5-6

CLASSIC EUROPEAN LYRICS –
Translated from the Gaelic, the French and the Spanish
ISBN: 978-0-9561435-6-3

COMMONWEALTH –
An Introduction to Business Economics
ISBN: 978-0-9561435-7-0

MISSING PERSONS –
Detective Felix O'Neill in a Crime Adventure
ISBN: 978-0-9561435-8-7

WEREWOLF MURDERS –
Detective Felix O'Neill in a Crime Adventure
ISBN: 978-0-9561435-9-4

WereWolf Murders

Detective Felix O'Neill in a Crime Adventure

DREW CARSON

Order from https://www.createspace.com/3849696

Legals

ISBN: 978-0-9561435-9-4

TABLE OF CONTENTS

CHAPTER ONE

An Old Friend Visits

It was early evening and darkness was gradually falling over the old graveyard. The shadows of the Virgin and the angels could still be seen guarding the tombstones of the dear departed.

The old graveyard was shadowy and sinister and almost encroached on the house of the local priest, Fr. Charles. The paths and walls were covered with tropical flowers and plants, ivy and overhanging weeping willow. The cypress trees were heavy with Spanish moss. Birds called and hooted grotesquely in the mangroves.

The surroundings were somber and mysterious giving the impression that the nearby inhabitants were vulnerable. They seemed to be dominated by the grim rays of the moon above the old churchyard.

From the church came the sound of slow and eerie, traditional organ music. Inside the presbytery was a private parlor where the mother of the local priest liked to sit in quiet contemplation. The parlor led to a kind of lounge-library. The furnishings were lavish and included large tables, chairs, bookcases and pillars in the mid room area. There was a small organ along the far wall. Large pot plants dominated the room. Portraits of revered churchmen looked down from the walls. The doors and windows were covered with heavy brocade curtains.

One evening the mother of the local priest was sitting alone in her parlor. Matilde was an elderly woman wearing a black dress with a white lace collar. Suddenly she heard a knock at the front door. It was Doloree the visiting nurse who was an old friend.

Doloree was thin, wizened and quite old. She was dressed in long, gray outdoor robes, white gloves and cowl.

As she entered the parlor, Doloree seemed edgy and uncomfortable and looked around nervously at times.

During their conversation, Elene the maid came and went at times to dust and arrange among the large furniture in the old-fashioned library.

Matilde was comfortable and at ease. She was pleasant and gracious as she greeted her visitor.

Matilde spoke in a gossipy, matter-of-fact manner, "The question is Doloree, Who and what is a werewolf? There is no question that there have been more than a few mysterious werewolf deaths around here in recent months and years. It's only now that it has become common knowledge but it has long been believed that a werewolf is walking at night."

Doloree leaned forward inquiringly. "You're making me nervous. Of course people, especially young people, do tend to leave these remote parts. Sometimes they just run off without warning their families. It's so thoughtless and selfish of them."

"I suppose that is true," responded Matilde, "but there have certainly been one or two terrible murders here recently. Bodies have been found torn apart."

"Heaven protect us," said Doloree in a state of shock. "I can't understand how a werewolf can live among Christians or just what kind of a creature it could be. I mean, Is it a man or a beast?"

As they talked, Elene the maid came and went inconspicuously.

Doloree was tense and continued to look around nervously.

"Well, as the mother of Fr. Charles you are certainly in a position to meet with many visitors as well as all the important people of the parish, so you must get some sort of opinions. As a simple religious and nurse I only meet the poor."

Then she smiled slightly, shrugged and shook her head.

"Of course I have heard a few rumors of killings in the outlying parts. However, I took the killings to be the work of bandits. Dear, dear, as you say Matilde, What exactly is a werewolf?"

Then speaking in a slightly sinister manner, "A kind of man-monster but is there really such a thing?"

"Fr. Charles is certainly worried about the killings and the presence of a werewolf," said Matilde. "He has warned me several times. Mother, he says, be careful whom you let into the presbytery. Something in disguise is finding its way into the homes of the people. Something is walking in the jungles and swamps. Be careful Mother, he says. Please promise me you will."

Again, unseen by the others Elene entered the room quietly to do some light dusting and arranging here and there.

Doloree stood up strangely looking around and listening carefully. Then she casually asked, "We are alone aren't we?"

"Certainly Doloree," responded Matilde, "and of course you may speak to me confidentially at any time if you have any problem. No one else will disturb us."

Doloree sat down again and smiled awkwardly with patent insincerity.

Then with hesitation in her voice, "Yes I am a little nervous. It is just, it is just these mysterious murders we were talking about. I suppose these horrible murders, mostly of women, have upset me more than I like to admit. I was, well, trying to play it down. But I must confess I am afraid. My work as you know, yes, my work as a nurse requires me to travel about at all hours of the day and night. So these random killings have disturbed me."

She looked concerned and worried as one bidding for sympathy.

Matilde responded to her with deep understanding, "Of course, how silly of me not to have thought of that. It must be terrifying for you. Here I am almost afraid to answer the door and yet I am safe and protected in the presbytery. For who would dare to enter a priest's home on an unlawful mission?

"My son Fr. Charles really does worry unnecessarily. And there you are out in the woods and highways at all hours of the day and night on call to almost anyone. It really must be terrible for you."

Doloree shiftily looked sideways.

"Yes Matilde. What is this werewolfism anyway?"

"No one is quite sure Doloree."

Then in a rather complacent manner, "It's nothing for you to worry about Doloree. I am sure that these creatures whatever they are, man or beast cannot harm any true Christian. I'm sure that our Lady always protects all of us, especially you religious on your good and godly visits to those who need you."

"Really Matilde. But then what do we actually know of the werewolf?"

"It's said to be a shapeshifter," replied Matilde with a confidential and informative air and still complacent.

"A what?" asked Doloree, staring at Matilde.

"A creature that changes its shape from man to beast or beast to man. I'm not sure which. But it is a master of disguise. That's how it comes at times into the homes of its victims. It can take on many different forms."

She stared at Doloree in quizzical contemplation, as Doloree looked stunned.

"Doloree are you sure?"

"Sure of what?" responded Doloree quickly and suspiciously.

"Are you sure that?" replied Matilde, "I'm not frightening you?"

Doloree smiled.

It was very clear that Matilde was not suspicious of Doloree.

Doloree continued to smile as she caressed her hair in a gesture of relief. "No Matilde, as one who travels a lot at night I need to know these things."

"Of course you do Doloree my dear. That's why I'm mentioning these rumors."

Then Matilde began to comment like a person trying to justify something dubious.

"You see I'm not trying to panic you, just trying to well, inform you so that you will be forewarned and forearmed."

"Of course," said Doloree primly, "just for my own safety. You are extremely well informed Matilde. I knew you would be and that's why I came to see you."

Matilde smiled warmly, "Yes exactly. Anyway where was I?"

"The shapeshifter," responded Doloree. "The master of disguise."

Matilde raised her hand and flicked it towards Doloree in a gesture that said, Of course I remember now. Yes indeed.

"Ah yes. I think that is just about the latest talk in the parish."

Then she raised the index finger of her waving hand to pinpoint the exact theme of her conversation.

"That was it, the disguiser. The fishing folk call him Zakotu. Some say that he is the reincarnation of an old spirit of the indigenos. He is the one who changes and now hides here and walks among us."

Suddenly Doloree stood up briefly. "How could such a creature hide? How could we not see it lurking among the trees or behind the furniture? It is impossible. A werewolf cannot just disappear. Surely we would be able to see it."

Matilde gently shook her head. "No, you don't understand. It's an impostor. It's an actor."

Then speaking to Doloree in a more determined manner, "You see it takes on different forms so that we do not recognize it."

Elene quietly left the room but made a slight noise in the course of her light chores.

Doloree heard the noise, stood up again and looked behind her puzzled. "Did I hear a noise? Are you sure we are alone?"

Matilde replied reassuringly, "I think so Doloree."

Doloree subtly and inconspicuously flexed her fingers claw-like at Matilde. However, she quickly sat down again as Matilde, unaware, turned her attention back to Doloree.

"These things are mysteries, Matilde."

Matilde sniffed the air and began to wonder if she smelled garlic. She wondered if someone had been cooking at that time of the evening. Surely not? Still, servants sometimes do their own thing.

Then responding to Doloree, "Yes, mysteries as you say. Of course, one can speculate but no one knows for sure. It's all part of the great mystery of the undead. The returners who live beyond the bounds of humanity."

"To kill others, Matilde?"

"Apparently," responded Matilde in some fear. "It is strange and weird. That's why it's good to know that maybe these mysteries will soon be solved by the scholars of good and evil who have come to the village to study all the murder and mutilation."

"Who and where?" asked Doloree with an increased interest.

"At the inn there is a young lady professor of natural science who has come to our little village to investigate the recent murder. She has been looking up tales of horror and has already written a book about some kind of a monster.

"The famous detective Felix O'Neill and his assistant Dr. Garzon have also arrived. Isn't it marvelous to think that all these experts are here to study the werewolf murders and to help us drive out the murderer from among us. Our little village is becoming quite infamous."

"Indeed, no wonder Matilde. The tales are strange."

Elene returned to the room on another routine task. She was quiet and unseen by the others.

Then Doloree stood up fairly close to Matilde and behind her leaning over her.

"Doloree that's funny. I seem to smell garlic. I wonder why? Anyway Doloree I see that you are anxious about these things."

Then in a kindly way, "Well, I am only an old lady. Fr. Charles has a book about werewolves that explains at least part of the mystery. It has to do with magic and rejuvenation by forbidden science. It is a terrible book Doloree but written by a saintly author for our protection. Indeed, it sets out a lot of facts about the werewolf. Would you like to read it? I'm sure it would be alright if I lent it to you."

"Thank you Matilde I would very much like to read the book."

"Well then, let me get it for you now."

Then Matilde stood up and went to the nearest bookshelf and began to scan the titles with her back to Doloree.

"Let me see now. Where is that book?"

Doloree assumed a posture of slight aggressiveness with her hands clawed and teeth bared just a little but relaxed again as Matilde turned around.

Matilde motioned to Doloree, "Please be seated Doloree. Do relax."

Doloree sat down briefly and nervously straightened up in the chair as Matilde turned back to the bookshelf.

"I'm sure there is no one to overhear us Doloree. Do not be nervous."

Elene did not hear the conversation as she quietly continued her dusting and arranging.

Matilde was engrossed in looking for the book as Doloree drew closer to her. She resumed her former hand-claw posture, ready-to-strike with greater ferocity than before and in complete silence but did not approach Matilde at first.

Suddenly Matilde called out with great satisfaction, "Ah, here it is. This is the book I was looking for."

While Matilde was occupied in her book-finding the moonlight had been briefly obscured by a cloud and suddenly Doloree had turned into a werewolf.

Matilde turned around with the book in her hand and gave out a loud scream in unbelief and sheer horror as the werewolf struck at Matilde from behind. She dropped the book as the werewolf came closer and seized her by the throat. Then Matilde fell behind a chair as the werewolf began to tear her apart. Matilde's screams were joined by the screams of Elene.

The werewolf paused for a moment and looked around as for another victim then hid behind a pillar and became silent for a while. It listened and hearing loud voices in the distance left the presbytery by way of the front door. The werewolf then quickly disappeared into the graveyard.

The growls and screams were heard outside in the grounds of the church. Suddenly Fr. Charles, a priest in full frock, appeared outside the church. He looked shocked and frightened at what he had just heard. Along with him came Elene's mother Janice the housekeeper. She was an old lady dressed in a long black gown.

They rushed into the presbytery and discovered the body of Matilde. Fr. Charles was distraught and prayed briefly in silence.

Elene emerged from hiding and wept uncontrollably for some time. After she had regained her composure, she slowly started to speak.

"Mother it was a werewolf. One minute Fr. Charles' mother was speaking to Sister Doloree the nurse and then all of a sudden the werewolf seized old Matilde. Oh dear heavens it was horrible."

Then Fr. Charles asked Elene what had happened to Sister Doloree?

"I don't know, Fr. Charles, she just seemed to disappear. The moon went down behind the clouds I think. The candles are not strong."

"Was Sister Doloree taken away by the werewolf then?" asked Janice.

"Maybe, I just don't know. I wasn't watching closely. I was hiding and listening in the silence after Matilde was killed."

"Think carefully now Elene," said Fr. Charles. "This is important. Were Doloree and the werewolf here at the same time? Or did Doloree run off when the werewolf arrived?"

Elene answered with tears streaming down her face, "Fr. Charles I just don't know. There was a horrible silence when I thought that the werewolf was listening to hear me breathing so as to kill me. I heard a sound like a swish of skirts as it fled. I'm sorry, I just don't know."

Elene and her mother stood weeping together for some time.

Fr. Charles walked away from the immediate murder scene to the center of the room and stared into space as in a state of shock.

"I did so try to be careful and yet somehow the werewolf was able to walk even into the house of the religious. Who knows, perhaps the werewolf was disguised as Doloree."

He put his hands to his eyes to suppress his weeping and shook his head.

"And I was just reading the words of the patriarch Job, Alas the thing that I greatly feared has come upon me. Something evil is walking in these swamps and jungles. No doubt it is a werewolf, a destroyer of the flock. But what?

"The question is, Who or what is the werewolf?"

CHAPTER TWO

A Touch of History

The great hall of the old abbey was full of bookshelves filled to overflowing with many large ecclesiastical, legal and scientific books.

On some of the tables there lay huge open volumes and piles of closed books as though someone had been studying or browsing. Some pens and ink and paper also lay on the tables. Traditional artifacts, artwork and tapestries hung from the walls.

On one of the walls was a screen which contained pictures of the nearby museum of confessions. In the distant past suspects and witnesses had been interrogated and intimidated prior to the trials that took place in the religious courts of orthodoxy. As a warning to the guilty, pictures of medieval torture such as the Screw, the Claw, the Rack, the Iron Maiden and the Spider hung on many of the walls.

There was a large barred window which formed part of the left wall of the chamber and three hangmen's nooses could be seen hanging in the yard outside.

The library was lit by candlelight as the abbess sat engrossed in poring over her books at one of the tables. She was an elderly woman of slight build and weight with a rather weak and wizened figure.

Following a loud knock at the front gate, a group of visitors were invited into the abbey. Canon Louis, Detective Felix O'Neill and his friend Dr. Garzon were immediately ushered into the library by two nuns, Sister Prudence and Sister Papillion. The nuns, dressed in long black robes, were more elderly and frail than the abbess. After they had introduced the group to the abbess they retired at once after bowing and kissing her hand.

The canon was a thin, stiff and mature man who wore a perpetually worried expression on his face as though weighed down by the burdens of law and exegesis. This was particularly noticeable by his chronic inability to believe anyone about anything.

Mr. Felix O'Neill was a lean, muscular, hawkish-looking man. He was dressed in long outdoor leggings, light tweed cloak, walking stick, robin-hood hat and strong walking boots.

He was followed by a Dr. Garzon, his right-hand man, who was broad-shouldered and rather stocky. Dr. Garzon sported a walrus moustache and sideburns and was slightly overweight but of a powerful build. He was dressed in brown tweeds.

Canon Louis as a lawyer of the church had also been called upon occasionally by secular authority to act as a magistrate on local minor misdemeanors.

These appointments were usually part-time and at the discretion of the abbess. However, they were nonetheless considered somewhat prestigious appointments as recognizing integrity, knowledge of law and status in the local areas.

The canon's look of innate concerned skepticism was accentuated by a tendency to shake his head slightly every few seconds. This was a purely nervous twitch but one that seemed always to communicate a subtly worried, negative message as if to say, No, I am afraid I can't quite accept that. That worries me and there must be some misunderstanding.

One wondered if this involuntary negativism was the result of long years of learnt skepticism in the tombs of justice. Or perhaps it was a mere nervous twitch, so suited to an inquisitional scholar that years ago it had been shrewdly recognized as a professional asset by his superiors and had resulted in his receiving the appointment of Canon of Law in the first place. It is sad to think that a twitch in the neck may be as good as a Masters Degree in Law but such is life.

Anyhow, he proceeded to introduce the visitors to the abbess. "Your highness, my dear Abbess, it is most gracious of you to grant us an audience."

As he spoke he shook his head, No, No, said the gesture.

"You are so deeply concerned about the welfare of your humble religious. You are so devoted to orthodoxy."

Again, No, No, he twitched.

"So keen to bring the murderer of the flock to justice."

The abbess interrupted him with a casual wave of the hand.

"Enough my dear Canon, time enough for a eulogy when I'm dead."

She smiled at Felix O'Neill.

"But that will not be for a little while, a few months yet I hope. I am old as you can see. Mr. O'Neill, you must be the author of several monographs on the secret sciences, Felix O'Neill the famous detective who has come here to help us solve the werewolf mystery murders."

She spoke in a pleasant tone. "I'm so pleased to see you. I hope that we can work together. I am the Abbess Concordee. You may be aware that our village's elevation here is just a little above the nearby swamps, bogs and jungles. I hope you will find it healthy. I want very much to solve these crimes against my people. I feel sure that we are getting closer to the truth.

"Earlier I asked Canon Louis here to arrange for the questioning of one of our nuns, Doloree a nurse, who unfortunately is our chief suspect at the moment."

Then she addressed Canon Louis, "She has gone missing from the abbey. Did you attend to this Canon Louis?"

Twitching negatively, he replied, "Yes your highness, I sent Sergeant Antoine to find her. I understand that she is in hiding. A sure sign of guilt."

"Or fear," suggested Felix O'Neill. "Or unsociability. Or desire for peace and quiet. Or being away visiting as a nurse. Or away seeking information. I myself have been absent many times for some of these reasons."

Canon Louis replied with a sinister and threatening sharpness of tone in his voice, "Guilt and fear of punishment is the most obvious reason."

Then he twitched No, No.

"Mr. O'Neill this chamber besides being a library is the higher ecclesiastical and traditional courtroom for this parish. Common crimes like theft and brawling and drunkenness and fraud and fighting are dealt with in the village courtroom. Graver matters like blasphemy, heresy, witchcraft, treason or assassination require a tribunal. Such serious religious crimes should be tried here by the parish tribunal of number one - the priest, number two - the canon-theologian, that is I myself and thirdly - the senior administrator of the local church, the abbess here."

"My dear Abbess," said Dr. Garzon, "your concern for a solution to this mystery is inspiring."

The abbess smiled inscrutably, "I am just a poor old lady at heart. It is the traditional role of the abbess to represent her nuns and the local poor."

Then with a humble tone in her voice, "After all I must help to protect the flock of local hard-working, honest, religious people who fish and shoot waterfowl for a living. I try to preserve our local culture and also protect the poor from the powers of darkness."

Then she pointed to the open books and the bookshelves, "That is why I study here. Of course my first duty is to direct the religious community of nuns - the convent."

Mr. O'Neill was interested and nodded. He looked curiously at some of the books.

"Indeed Abbess I see that you are engaged in deep theology, hmm, St. John Chrysostom and St. Augustine. All very orthodox and praiseworthy I'm sure."

The abbess was pleased, "Thank you Mr. O'Neill."

Suddenly there was heard the sound of scuffling and shouting. Then the two nuns sisters Papillion and Prudence entered and bowed to the abbess.

"Sergeant Antoine has arrived with a lost sister," said Sister Papillion.

The sergeant entered the library. He was of mature age and swarthy with black hair and white teeth. Sergeant Antoine, bumbling and officious, was dressed in military fashion as he pushed Doloree with her hands tied behind her back.

As he pushed Doloree ahead of him, he shouted, "The guilty one has been found. I myself discovered the hiding place in an old boathouse surrounded by cats."

He abusively taunted Doloree, "Rider of broomsticks and changer into cats."

Then he scratched his head as he consulted his thoughts on the matter. "No - dogs. Oh, we have you now witch. Brewer of magic stew."

Doloree shouted naively, "Lies, lies, all lies. Such terrible lies."

The Abbess Concordee interrupted her and spoke to the sergeant imperiously.

"Silence Antoine, it is for me as Mother Superior not you to decide this sister's guilt or innocence."

Sergeant Antoine paused and bowed obsequiously and remembered to remove his hat.

"Indeed your superiorness, forgive my enthusiasm ma'am and gentlemen. You see it's my duty as an honest policeman."

The abbess calmly interrupted, "Quiet Sergeant. You may leave. This sister is now back in her rightful home. It is our decision that you leave now. Is that not so Canon Louis?"

Canon Louis twitched negatively, No, No, and then murmured, "Yes, oh yes indeed Mother Superior."

Sergeant Antoine backed out bowing and scraping towards the floor and showing his teeth but it was not clear if he was sincere or sarcastic.

The abbess watched him carefully as he withdrew.

"Canon Louis, thank you for taking over," shouted Sergeant Antoine. "Put her to death. She's guilty. She's a witch. She scratched me on the nose. Kill her off like a dog. She's a wolf-dog. A scratching witch."

As he left the room he pointed with his hat towards Doloree.

"No, No, I am not a witch," pleaded Sister Doloree. "I am not guilty. I have done no harm. I have hurt no one."

"Prudence, my dear Prudence, bring Pierre here at once," ordered the abbess.

Prudence bowed and left the library to find Pierre.

"Mr. O'Neill, Pierre is the curator of our museum and is one of our historians on witches and heresy."

Then she pointed to several pictures on the walls of the library.

"He is very much an expert on the local workings of the inquisition and how to deal with possible apostates."

Felix O'Neill became astounded and incredulous, "Witches? Surely if this poor woman had supernatural powers she would have wounded the sergeant with more than a scratch on the nose?"

"We must be careful," said the abbess, who was superstitiously cautious. "It is said that the strength of a werewolf comes and goes according to such things as spells and potions and movements of the moon and stars. We do know that Sister Doloree had at least deserted the abbey."

Eventually Sister Prudence returned with Pierre who was a hunchback.

Pierre was thickset and weak-faced. He was pale but cheerful, powerful but soulless. Dressed in a curator's uniform with cap and thick waist belt, he strutted rather than walked and was arrogant and self-confident on the surface but fragile and fearsome underneath.

He bowed, "Mother Superior, Canon Louis, ladies and gentlemen, I am at your service."

The abbess pointed to Doloree, "Sister Doloree here has been absent from the abbey without permission and so is a suspect in certain crimes. Your knowledge of the crimes and apostasies of oldentimes may be of help in this matter."

Pierre bowed again and went down on one knee beside Doloree who held her bound hands behind her back but still kept her head low as she knelt.

"Doloree my child," said the abbess, "a poor woman was killed last night. She was Matilde, the priest's mother. You were seen at the priest's house speaking to Matilde last night at the time when she was killed. This was no ordinary murder to be tried at common court. This was a murder by a witch or wizard, for the form of the werewolf was seen. Divine laws may well have been broken, so we must seek to inquire if you are guilty or have any guilty knowledge. Do you understand?"

Sister Prudence laughed and chortled as she pointed to the three nooses outside the window. "See the lovely view from our little museum."

Sister Papillion chortled as she rubbed her hands together with keenness. "Yes and looking at those old pictures may also encourage you to tell what's true - hee, hee - give us a clue."

Felix O'Neill glanced unpleasantly at the sisters and at the pictures of the inquisition and the three nooses hanging in the courtyard outside the window.

"Ma'am," said Doloree, "I understand that these werewolf killings are the work of demons and wizards. But I know nothing of them. I am just an old nurse. All last night I was attending a sickbed several miles away from the house of the priest where this terrible murder took place.

"I know nothing of the murder and I have never murdered anyone. Someone must have been pretending to be me. I am innocent. Please Mother, you are the only protector of us poor religious in these remote swamplands and jungles. Please let me be sent back to my work."

But the abbess made no response as Doloree continued to plead in desperation.

"The sick ones I visited are witnesses for me that I was there with them last night. I was not even near the house of Fr. Charles. I was ten miles away. I was told by the family of the sick that I was a suspect and the police were looking for me. So I hid nearby in fear, not guilt."

"That is easily checked on," said Felix O'Neill. "My friend and I will do so."

The abbess interrupted in a pleasant tone of voice, "One moment Mr. O'Neill, this is our responsibility not yours. Let our usual inquiry process be observed. We have local contacts and will pass all findings on to you."

Felix O'Neill was surprised at this and upset but self-controlled, "Of course."

"My dear Abbess," added Dr. Garzon, "if anyone in the world can help it will be

Felix O'Neill, the world's greatest consulting detective."

"We understand that you are here to help us Mr. O'Neill," responded the abbess in a diplomatic manner. "However, our local law requires that where the testimony of the accused differs from that of the accuser then the accused must be put to a test."

"No, No, No," cried Doloree. "There is no reason. Why can my witnesses not be called to testify?"

The abbess responded smoothly but in a hostile manner, "Your witnesses will be called, my dear. But you are making things difficult for us. You will also be questioned and soon."

"Oh no. Not that," cried Doloree.

O'Neill became puzzled, concerned and suspicious. "Not what?"

At this point in the proceedings the abbess told Pierre to take Doloree to the old museum.

"Pierre, take her to the Chamber of Confessions and keep her there."

She raised her finger in caution, "But do not question her yet."

Pierre shook his head, absently.

"No, No. I would never do that Mother Superior. It is not for me to question a religious."

Then the abbess pointed to Papillion and Prudence, "Dear sisters, you should speak to her about these questions. These inconsistencies between her tale and those of the priest and Elene. They all say that they saw her last night in the presbytery when the priest's mother was murdered."

Sisters Papillion and Prudence smiled and bowed.

Pierre pulled Doloree as she screamed and resisted. But he continued all the more to push and pull her by the arms as he dragged her towards the old museum.

"What is going on here?" asked Felix O'Neill. "Where exactly are you taking this woman?"

The Abbess Concordee remained silent and contemptuous for a few moments but then responded to Felix O'Neill.

"Merely to the old museum as a mere reminder of the church's ability to find out the truth in times past."

Canon Louis twitched No, No.

"The normal process," he said, "is to interrogate and persuade suspects to tell the truth. We cannot just take their word that they are innocent and then release them. They must be subject to some kind of inquisitional routine. Of course we cannot and would not use force today but we can use a little psychology to, perhaps, just look at the former implements of truth-seeking."

Dr. Garzon was horrified.

"I hope you don't mean some form of intimidation. Surely you can't mean threats or scares? An old woman would confess to anything under threat."

Felix O'Neill nodded but remained cool and suspicious.

The abbess looked towards Mr. O'Neill and Dr. Garzon and tried to calm their concerns.

"Of course we don't mean threats. Just a subtle reminder."

Sister Prudence bowed and squirmed. "Thank you, Mother Superior."

Then she looked at Felix O'Neill, "Thank you. We will take care of our sister. Her gentle sisters alone will inquire of her concerning these matters."

"My dear gentlemen," said the abbess, "you must understand that here we have a traditional rural setting. I must remind you both that this is all within my personal jurisdiction as an abbess. There have been horrible murders, apparently a werewolf, certainly cold-blooded killing. Our people respond to the traditional procedures, just as Doloree responded a few minutes ago with fear. In this way actual torture is never necessary. The old torture machines are only a tourist and student attraction - at most a psychological reminder. Of course they are never used in reality."

Then evasively, "All that is needed is the fear of the consequences of lying and what do we get? We get what we want, what you want and what all of human civilization has sought for centuries. All that we need for justice and honor and for the making of an orderly life. Then the good can live freely and the wicked can be punished. All that we need for civilization to continue, the truth.

"My dear Mr. O'Neill and Dr. Garzon we could not, we simply could not, get this truth simply by asking for it. We need to work for it, perhaps by craft, by cunning or even by trickery. Maybe at times by some slight or little white deception. But in any case, by all means possible to get at that truth so that justice can be achieved."

Then dreamily and intently as one seeing visions, "Justice can only be reached through the road of truth because justice is the result of truth, the child of truth. Truth can only be achieved by hard work. It does not come easily. So let us not condemn the traditional ways of finding out the truth. Truth treads a lonely road. Lies have many convivial friends."

Dr. Garzon spoke up, "But those old machines that you showed Doloree, whether they work or not, whether in a museum or not, were once used to harm people and cause pain. Is this a good image for a body of religious, a community of prayer?"

"Mr. O'Neill and Dr. Garzon," replied the abbess, "I have here many volumes written by the saints that say they flogged themselves. They had themselves flogged in order to come to a knowledge of the truth. The greatest saints in the history of the church. Shall I recall their lives to you?"

But Felix O'Neill replied sharply, "No, ma'am. I am quite aware of the voluntary self-discipline of the early saints but this is not self-discipline nor is it voluntary."

The abbess was a little taken aback. "No, but we try to find out what really happened not by traditional methods but by a reminder of such. This is better than merely asking malefactors to voluntarily admit their crimes.

"Surely you do not believe in merely asking them, Are you a murderer? Answer No. Very well, you are free to go. Surely there must be more to it than this. Remember gentlemen that we are a remote religious community. We do not have any scientific laboratories to sift evidence or analyze soil or blood or bones or skin. We need some kind of objectivity."

"Well yes," responded Felix O'Neill. "You need honest and impartial witnesses. Good, objective evidence, for instance."

"And if these are not forthcoming what then?" asked the abbess. "The killer walks free? Please bear with us."

"Look Abbess Concordee," said Felix O'Neill, "I am here only at the invitation of a person who wishes to remain unnamed - an investigator. I do hope that I can help you all to achieve the safety and the law and order you wish to achieve. Please grant me one favor."

"But of course Mr. O'Neill," replied the abbess in her pleasant tone of voice. "I too wish to restore law and order. What is your favor? Would you and Dr. Garzon wish to be our guests here at the abbey?"

"Thank you Abbess but I need to be among the poor people and the victims to receive information. But if you could promise me that no one will be charged or accused. Please do nothing until I have had a chance, with others help no doubt, to find out by proper evidence and witnesses just what is going on here. And who or what is responsible."

"You have my promise Mr. O'Neill. Some persons may need to be counseled a little for that is the established disciplinary practice here. But I can certainly promise you that no one will come to any harm within my jurisdiction until they have been counseled in front of impartial witnesses. And you may be in attendance here."

She pointed towards some chairs, "At any time you wish. You have my word on this as Mother Abbess."

"Thank you Madam Abbess. Then I will waste no more time in trying to help solve these mysteries."

Then Felix O'Neill drew together his cloak, his hat and walking stick.

"Thank you for your courtesy."

The abbess smiled and shook hands with Mr. O'Neill and Dr. Garzon.

"And I will look forward to hearing of your progress."

Then speaking in her relaxed and leisurely way, "Goodbye gentlemen."

Felix O'Neill and Dr. Garzon said goodbye to the abbess then bowed as they left the room.

In the distance the faint voice of Doloree could be heard as she continued to plead, "No, No, I have never killed anyone. I am not a witch."

CHAPTER THREE
Who is the Werewolf?

Madame La Professeur Vermillion was staying at the local inn. Her particular area of expertise was the life sciences. She had made a prior arrangement to meet the other investigators in the churchyard that was located to the front of the church and close by the crypt.

Professor Vermillion was young, alert and petite but somewhat eccentric in her appearance. She was shortsighted and had to wear glasses. A keen and intellectual person, she was in the habit of continually removing her glasses to wipe and adjust them.

Soon Felix O'Neill and his friend Dr. Garzon entered the churchyard.

At the same time Anne, the hostess of the local inn, found a seat nearby to read a book.

Mr. O'Neill was dressed in his usual attire and both men wore hats which they promptly removed out of reverence for the dead. They retained their traveling cloaks and walking sticks. The mature Dr. Garzon was now wearing a white suit, white shirt and bow tie.

As she arrived at the churchyard, Professor Vermillion approached Dr. Garzon and detective Felix O'Neill. They all greeted each other and shook hands. The churchyard was a little overclouded by the eerie atmosphere of the graves. As they talked quietly in front of the church, there was a slight rumble of thunder.

"I am Dr. Arturo Garzon, healtharian and homeopath, a former health officer in the mercantile marine."

Then Garzon proceeded to introduce Felix O'Neill to Professor Vermillion.

"Madame Vermillion is a professor of natural science. My friend Mr. O'Neill is a master detective. Like Madame Vermillion I am also researching for a novel on the supernatural. From what I have read of the professor our interests are the same - the occult. But I am quite interested in a spiritual approach to witchcraft although novels essentially provide entertainment and amusement about the occult."

"Well, of course novels are more than fun," said Felix O'Neill. "Some novelists predict, others inform, some are scientific, some change society."

"On the other hand," responded Professor Vermillion, "science also has its myths and honored falsehoods."

"Quite so," said Felix O'Neill. "I must agree Madame la Professeur."

The professor looked up at the sky in awe. "Sky grumble."

Dr. Garzon was puzzled, "Beg pardon ma'am?"

"That is the local proverbial comment for thunder and drums – a bad day for the fearful," replied Professor Vermillion.

"Yes, alas for the fearful victims but my friend Mr. Felix O'Neill is probably the world's greatest detective. His brain and his intuitive powers are second to none. The killer's days are drawing to a close.

"However in any case I am also interested in the humanitarian and healing aspects of any discipline," continued Dr. Garzon. "That is why I thought we should meet here beside the church. Many of the appearances and attacks of the werewolf have taken place in the homes and roads near this old graveyard."

"I seek a scientific and non-magical explanation of why this old graveyard should be involved," said Felix O'Neill. "My investigations are carried out primarily to meet an intellectual challenge but also to help make this world a better place."

"I am interested in the strange and unusual in natural science," responded Professor Vermillion. "In fact, one of my recent interests is pathology. The man-wolf may be a pathological mutant and this is a rare chance to study one so extraordinary."

"So you study freaks Professor?" asked a surprised Felix O'Neill.

"Well yes," she admitted, "the freak represents the sick man of creation. What makes its mind work and why does it act as it does? Some scientists wish only to understand the way individuals survive but I seek to lay the foundations for the ultimate healing of many in order to set the whole man in a healthy world and that necessitates the study of genetic deviants.

"I am very pleased to meet both of you. It's good to know that I am not the only one investigating these mysterious werewolf murders. Let's share our knowledge and suspicions and ideas for just a moment."

Felix O'Neill was visibly pleased and gratified. "Absolutely, we may learn from each other, Professor."

"Yes, I understand that both you Mr. O'Neill and you Dr. Garzon have visited the local abbey."

"Indeed," replied Felix O'Neill, "and you may be interested to know that I have already checked out Doloree's alibi this afternoon. Several persons have told me that Doloree was visiting the sick some miles away at the time of the murder. The priest's housekeeper and servants are adamant that Doloree was there at the time of the werewolf murder of the priest's mother."

"Ah, here is a mystery that needs investigating," exclaimed the professor.

"Well, I have been working on a theory for some time," said Felix O'Neill, "and the fact of Doloree being in two places at the same time appears to confirm my theory."

"What theory, Mr. O'Neill?" asked the professor.

"Well, according to our known science it is impossible to impersonate anyone in appearance and voice and personality to such an extent as to fool old friends. But I believe that werewolves are advanced masters in the arts of disguise.

"It's just unbelievable that the werewolf would reveal its true identity so easily as to call at someone's front door as Doloree did, be identified by several good witnesses and then change its appearance and murder someone."

Then O'Neill spoke in a more deliberate and cold manner, "So it follows that the person acting in the face and shape of Doloree, a harmless old nun and nurse, was someone or something else."

All this time Anne the hostess of the inn had been sitting nearby reading a book. She looked up alertly interested at these words and began to pay attention.

She rose to her feet, "Forgive me for interrupting but, well, what I was going to say was there's a girl here who works for me at the inn. Her boyfriend was killed by the werewolf and she tells a very strange tale of the werewolf's apparent disguise. If you wish, I will ask her to speak to you. She may help you. Please forgive me. Do not let me interrupt. I'm very happy to have you all here as guests at my inn and I'll do all I can to help you."

She bowed to the others then returned briefly to her reading.

Felix O'Neill thanked her.

"Thank you Anne, I would be most interested to hear the girl's story."

Then he looked at the others.

"In fact, I am sure that disguise is the key to the mystery and not merely an ordinary disguise but rather a high level of metamorphosis or shapeshifting."

"To me as a scientist," commented Professor Vermillion, "metamorphosis is not an acceptable explanation. It smacks of the supernatural."

"Not at all Professor," said Felix O'Neill. "It's a very natural process. But of course too advanced for the scientists of today to quite understand."

"But not too difficult for an imaginative detective to grasp?" replied the professor in a pleasant tone.

O'Neill ignored the irony, "Exactly. Creative investigators and writers always are eras ahead of scientists."

Professor Vermillion shrugged, raised her eyebrows and wiped her glasses.

"Well O'Neill my dear fellow," said Dr. Garzon, who had been listening intently to the debate, "in my slight and superficial studies of sorcery and witchcraft I have come across those who sell their soul to the devil in order to gain power over others. And certainly the power to delude others and to hide by disguise is a very great power indeed."

"This all points to my theory that here we deal with a shapeshifter," remarked Felix O'Neill. "I fear that the werewolf is a master of murderous disguise who peddles a deadly and diabolical delusion."

Professor Vermillion interrupted with her take on the situation.

"Dr. Garzon with all due regard to your religious beliefs and Mr. O'Neill with every respect to your scientific analysis and strong investigative imagination, can I humbly just point out that there is a disease of the genes known as lycanthropy or werewolfism. Also, it is well established that the full moon exercises a tyrannical power over the minds and bodies of humans.

"Lunatics are those who are over-sensitive to Luna - the moon. The tides are subject to the moon, so also are our bodies and our minds. If a person has somehow been born with wolf-genes or by some similar misplacement of nature, then surely the wolf or other animal in the human will spring out at the time of the full moon."

Felix O'Neill calmly asked, "Why?"

Professor Vermillion was at a loss, "Why? Why? Why? Because it is a time when the mind is weak."

"Really?" exclaimed O'Neill. "So when the wolfman's mind is weak he turns into a wolf - a very, very strong animal. How can that be?"

Professor Vermillion continued, "You Mr. O'Neill are into mere theory. For your so-called science has never been accepted by any scientific school. And you sir, Dr. Garzon, are into magic. My explanation of lycanthropy is a known inherited disease."

Then Dr. Garzon shook his head in disapproval.

"The wolfman is a child of devilry not a chance mismatch of nature. Truly the wolf is an unlucky omen, death, disaster, doom. The Good Book says - Beware of false prophets in sheep's clothing but inwardly they are ravening wolves. And again - Ravening wolves will enter in among you, not sparing the flock."

The professor looked at all present including Anne the hostess who sat close by taking a keen interest in the proceedings, then she continued with her analysis.

"You realize, Mr. O'Neill, that if there is any truth in your theories at all and I do not know that there is, that almost anyone could be the werewolf?"

"Including you," remarked O'Neill.

"Exactly," the professor agreed. "There are a lot of suspects."

Felix O'Neill spread his hands, "I never suggested otherwise."

Then he pointed out in a pedagogical way, "All I ever suggested was that the werewolf is a creature of advanced science not magic or demons, not a matter of nature or genetic disorder. That is why I am very anxious to hear about the experience of the kitchenmaid who seems to have seen something of the werewolf's ability to change its shape."

Professor Vermillion concurred, "Yes, can we agree to bring her here to the church and talk to her? There are too many prying eyes and ears at the inn."

"Of course," said Felix O'Neill. "I'm sure that her experience would help to prove that my theory is at least a viable possibility."

Dr. Garzon and Mr. O'Neill nodded their approval.

Then Anne, the hostess of the inn, spoke to the group again.

"The canon and the Chief of Police are quite nearby. I can send for them. At this time of day they are usually free. Do you want me to fetch the girl whose boyfriend was killed by the werewolf? Her name is Blanche. Believe me, her testimony just about shows the truth of what you have been saying Mr. O'Neill."

Felix O'Neill smiled, "Of course, bring her here and please also send for the constable and the canon."

Anne went off to get Blanche and the others.

Dr. Garzon continued with his analysis of the situation.

"I feel sure that the devil, the selling of souls, with his sorcery and magic is the basis of the terror. The devil lies behind all evil and these killings are evil. No contrary testimony of a kitchenmaid need be taken seriously."

"I'm not so sure," argued the professor. "As a clinical scientist, I wouldn't completely dismiss any possibility, either magic or shapeshifting but I do suspect that a simple natural explanation is going to prove to be the answer to the mystery. We do need to remember that lycanthropy has been accepted for many centuries as a disease, the man-wolf syndrome – a form of chimera by natural dysfunction."

"Then why are there not similar mistakes with fish or fowl or cats or horses? All this is mere mythology," pointed out O'Neill. "So you're both wrong, as educated people, minds on rails, usually are. You realize that you are both traditionalists thinking of magic or nature and neither is the true answer. The werewolf is simply an advanced scientist. However, let's hear what this young kitchenmaid Blanche has to say. She is a victim of the werewolf and must know something."

Professor Vermillion then reminded the others, "Before we hear any witnesses we should remember that three people run this town - the abbess, the priest and the canon. Indeed the three are just about all of law and order in this village. If we are going to achieve any kind of justice or honest solution to the mystery of these werewolf murders we will need their help."

"Do you mean for purposes of getting cooperation from the public?" asked Felix O'Neill. "The help would be dubious I suspect."

"Well O'Neill, perhaps up to a point," remarked Dr. Garzon.

He nodded towards the professor.

"What Professor Vermillion suggests may have some validity."

Then he lowered his voice and glanced around. "However, Canon Louis is on his way and the canon is hardly the strongest personality, unless he's a great actor and fooling us."

Dr. Garzon lowered his voice this time to a whisper so as not to be overheard. "Speak of the devil."

Sure enough, Canon Louis came along accompanied by Sergeant Antoine.

As usual the canon was shaking his head and twitching No, No - it can't be true.

"Professor Vermillion and gentlemen, my compliments," said Canon Louis. "How are you all? I understand you have new evidence."

"Not quite sir," said Felix O'Neill, "but Anne our hostess is introducing a new witness to one of the recent werewolf murders. She is Blanche whose boyfriend was murdered."

"Yes I know. Michel her escort was murdered by the werewolf out there beyond the graveyard. But I don't understand why Sergeant Antoine and I have been sent for."

The canon continued twitching No, No. "Blanche is in no way a new witness. She gave full testimony before my court in my capacity as coroner."

Then he shrugged and looked mystified and twitched again. "Sergeant Antoine, you also have heard her testimony in court, isn't that so?"

Sergeant Antoine looked blank.

"I don't remember sir. To tell you the truth, sir, I'm only here to arrest people, if that is what you want, your honor."

He stood back, spread his hands and then grinned broadly.

"Show me the villain, the murderer, werewolf suspect, creature of terror and I will seize him."

He growled and strangled an imaginary suspect.

"Trust me, ma'am, sirs, your honor. I would arrest my own mother if ordered to. Although that would somewhat upset me."

At first he looked sad and then his voice uplifted as one in great generosity of spirit.

"Since I have almost forgiven her for my upbringing and I still retain some small glimmer of liking for the ugly old hag."

He put his hand on his heart. "Yes, I still almost feel a little soft spot for her despite all her insults to me growing up. Yes, I would arrest anyone."

Then he laughed loudly, "Including any of the four of you. Ha, Ha – just joking but true all the same."

Canon Louis shrugged in distaste at the outburst.

"In my work I find people like you Sergeant necessary but revolting."

Sergeant Antoine bowed and grinned.

"Thank you, thank you, your honor."

He touched his temple.

"I appreciate the compliment Canon Louis."

Then with an air of modesty, "I do my best. Yessir I do my best, sir, to be as you say, revolting against the ancient regime.

Vive la Commonwealth"

Canon Louis appeared mystified and twitched violently as the others looked on stunned at this incredible tirade from Sergeant Antoine.

CHAPTER FOUR

An Eyewitness Speaks

The debate still continued on among the others in the churchyard.

While they were all engrossed in their discussion, Anne the innkeeper arrived with Blanche a solemn young girl dressed in long servant's clothes. Blanche was shy and nervous as she bowed, curtsied to the company, then frowned unhappily.

Sergeant Antoine kissed the hand of Anne as he raised his hat extravagantly.

Anne introduced the girl to the others.

"This is Blanche, everyone."

Then she addressed Blanche in a kind and coaxing manner, "Blanche you are here among friends, please relax. These visitors, as you may know, are staying at the inn where we both work. They are searching for the murderer of your friend Michel."

Anne paused and looked quizzically at Blanche.

"May they succeed in their aims? They want only to know the full story of the murder incident - just as you told it to me."

Then she assured Blanche in a soft tone of voice, "No one will blame you for having been afraid to tell the whole story before. It must have put you into a state of shock. Isn't that true Canon?"

Canon Louis twitched negatively, No, No, definitely not, No, No.

"Yes Anne, the young girl was clearly shocked. It's time now to hear the whole story," he said.

Blanche relaxed somewhat but still looked unhappy.

"If I thought I was going to be believed I wouldn't hesitate to fill in some details.

She looked guiltily at Canon Louis then looked down at the ground.

Canon Louis resigned himself to her attitude.

"Very well child. Let us hear your fully detailed story. Better late than never."

Then he twitched again.

"My hope is to find out the truth from whoever, for whatever reason or whenever I can. Please tell."

Blanche spoke with hesitation in her voice.

"This may show that Doloree was not the werewolf," she said.

"Well, that may be," responded the canon, "but Doloree has confessed."

Professor Vermillion shook her head sadly then suddenly decided to interrupt.

"Only under threats, I fear."

Throughout these proceedings Felix O'Neill and Dr. Garzon had been quietly listening and taking careful note of all the comments and the all important body language of the participants. As Professor Vermillion added her opinion, they glanced at each other with raised eyebrows and a nod of the head which indicated their agreement on this point.

Then O'Neill spoke up, "Or worse, under torture perhaps."

Anne encouraged Blanche to continue.

"Please tell them what you told me Blanche."

At this point Blanche was in tears.

"Please let me pull myself together first before I continue."

She paused, put her head in her hands and knelt down in obvious mental turmoil.

"It was the day Michel and I thought would be as happy as any in our lives. We were in love. We went deep into the forest, just the two of us and Bobbin our little pack-donkey to pluck wild fruit and berries or maybe find some game. We were so happy with each other and eventually we followed the berries and herbs into this old churchyard where many do not go due to fear of the dead. Berries were plentiful then.

"The open hillside having been well worked, little by little we worked our way through the graveyard. We plucked some fruit and berries and put it in the pack-saddle on Bobbin the mule. Then hand and hand we strolled through the trees and graves and bushes for a while. It was summer and near noonday. Michel began to feel tired but I was too happy, too active and thoughtful to need a rest. I just wanted to stay awake for ever and think about our future life together."

She sobbed and then continued her story with her voice breaking up as she spoke.

"Anyway, Michel lay down among some shaded bushes while I danced and walked just a littleways away to pluck some flowers. I was never more than forty or fifty yards away from Michel, at the most. Though I could not see him, I knew that he was resting nearby so I was not afraid.

"Just as I began to feel really pleased with my bouquet, suddenly the sounds of terror pierced my ears. Birds cried out and squirrels screeched in fear. Then I heard the howling and growling of a dog or wolf and the screams of Michel coming from the place where he had laid down to rest. I dropped the flowers and screamed - Michel are you all right?

"At first I was petrified and could not move. I thought that perhaps a water-creature had strayed from the waterways but it was more like the ravening and snarling of a great dog, mixed with the terror of small creatures and birds. I heard Michel cry Blanche, the gun, get the gun. The gun.

"His voice was overwhelmed by the wolf sounds as I ran to Bobbin the donkey and seized the old game shotgun out of the saddlebag. I ran back towards the scene of the attack.

"From the ravening and growling noises and shouts I knew that Michel had at least been seriously wounded and I was determined to save him if I could. So I carefully made my way towards the place of the attack, pointing the gun.

"Suddenly the figure of Michel rose up out of the bushes, almost like one walking on air. I was just as terrified of this as I had been at the sounds of the wolfening and screaming and carnage. He seemed so calm, so deadly calm and relaxed. Even the birds became silent. I heard only a swishing sound as of a cloak or skirts moving and smelt a strange herbal smell in the air. I stopped and pointed the gun at the apparition. For at that time I felt sure it was Michel's ghost.

"A voice that sounded like Michel's told me to put down the gun. The voice said, It's only me, Michel. What is the matter? Put away the gun Blanche.

"I could not believe that Michel had not heard the screaming. Then he looked at me strangely and beckoned to me with his left hand.

"The voice told me to come. Blanche come here. Give me the gun. Do not shoot. I am unharmed. I am safe. All is well.

"He was so calm, unperturbed even-voiced. He was smiling handsomely like one undisturbed. The birds were still silent. I backed off, still pointing the game gun at him or his apparition but he continued to beckon strangely towards me.

"Come here Blanche. There's nothing wrong. Why are you pointing that gun at me?

"I just could not believe that Michel had not heard the screaming and wolf howls. I could not believe that he had not been harmed so I continued to back off, pointing the gun at where Michel had been sleeping so peacefully. Then, as the image of Michel began to disappear, I backed off onto the country road near the abbey. Fortunately, Sergeant Antoine happened to be passing at that time."

CHAPTER FIVE

Sergeant Antoine's Version

"Sergeant Antoine approached me and asked, What is the matter ma'am? Why the gun? Have you been attacked dear lady? Can I help you?

"I was so confused and afraid but I went with him to where Michel had been resting and from where the wolf howls and screams had come.

"Truly, the image of Michel that spoke to me had been a fantasy. For sure enough, even as I had feared, we found not only that Michel was dead but that his poor bones had been scattered all around."

Blanche sobbed as she spoke.

"Yes, his body torn to pieces and flung apart as by a wild animal, destroyed and half devoured as by a wolf or other wild creature just as the horrible noises had seemed to say.

"Ripped apart as by a savage monster. Michel had always been so handsome and alive. He was so kind and gentle and witty.

Now he was just a heap of things, like broken parts of a clock but who broke it? That's what I need to know. That's why I'm telling you this in the hope that it will help you to find out about what has become a complete and total nightmare to me.

"The sergeant and I looked at the murder scene and drew back in dread. I just stood there with the gun in my hand."

Blanche finished her story and stood in silence now as the others continued in their former mood of discussion.

Felix O'Neill was the first to break the silence.

"Blanche can you remember how long it was from the time you saw Michel beckoning to you until you and Sergeant Antoine found his body?"

"I don't know but it could not have been more than a couple of minutes."

"Sergeant Antoine what do you think?" asked O'Neill.

"How can I tell? I dunno. All I know is that I was on my horse on routine guard patrol. I heard a great cry from the birds that hoot and call and then I see Blanche holding a gun and walking backwards. So I stop the horse. She cries werewolf and murder and I follow her and I see a body torn up."

He shrugged and shook his head.

"A tragedy of horrors. Little pieces scattered here and there of someone, no doubt Michel, well and truly destroyed. If only it had been my mother instead. I could have breathed easy but no."

Then with bitterness in his voice, "It was an innocent person. Just an innocent human being. Surely this proves that destiny cannot exist. Surely this proves my point that destiny is a myth."

Canon Louis was more solemn and vindictive.

"Sergeant, blasphemy is still an offense in this country and in this jurisdiction. Are you aware of this?"

Sergeant Antoine flamboyantly waved his arms.

"Everybody in this village is an atheist except those who make a living from the status quo."

"What exactly do you mean by status quo?" asked Felix O'Neill.

"The land-owning and job-holding and government payroll status quo, Mr. O'Neill. What other status quo is there?"

Then he shouted defiantly.

"This country is a commonwealth. I am an atheist. It is my right. We are not under the ancient regime so why should I be interrogated in this way?"

"Sergeant Antoine, please do not misunderstand me," explained Felix O'Neill quietly, "I was not interrogating you. I ask only as an outsider for information. Now I know that landowning or renting out land or taking a government payout amounts to an establishment."

O'Neill counted up to three on his fingers and then continued.

"These three things equal the status quo in this swampland, right?"

"That is it sir," replied the sergeant. "Land, government contracts or a taxpayer-paid job - that's corruption - the status quo. See sir? Look, I'm sorry. I am on edge. I worry about these werewolf murders. The body of Michel destroyed tore me apart just as much as the werewolf tore him apart."

He shook his head.

"We must catch this werewolf and kill it. It's a tragedy. No one ever deserved, no one on earth ever deserved to be torn apart in that way."

Then he started to rub his chin and appeared to be in deep contemplation about everything.

"Except maybe my mother."

Then he brightened.

"But then, ha, ha, retribution will come to her also, if life is just."

Then he became sad and despondent again.

"But then life is not only not just, it is not even good. So what good is that?"

He spread his hands and looked miserable.

"It's all a mess. It's all a terrible mess."

Professor Vermillion looked at Sergeant Antoine with interest, a long look up and down just as a zoologist might look at a specimen.

"Hmm," she thought.

The others gazed at each other in utter disbelief.

"Lady Professor, what is the problem?" asked the sergeant.

However, Professor Vermillion did not answer him but turned her attention to Blanche.

"Err, I am just wondering how to explain the apparition of Michel immediately after his murder," she queried.

Felix O'Neill ventured an explanation.

"The few minutes between the time of the apparition and the finding of his body by Antoine and Blanche would hardly have been enough to allow for such a terrible murder and mutilation and cannibalism.

"Therefore, Michel was dead when he appeared to Blanche. Besides, he appeared to Blanche after an apparent vicious werewolf attack. So who was the actor impersonating him? Obviously it was the murderer for I do not believe in ghosts."

"No, me either sir," added Sergeant Antoine as he nodded eagerly. "It's bad enough to be scared by them without having to believe in them."

Canon Louis twitched negatively at the sergeant who saluted him defiantly.

Then Felix O'Neill spoke more slowly, "Therefore, since dead and mutilated men cannot stand up, it was not Michel who stood up."

Blanche sobbed.

"I know Mr. O'Neill. I have wondered and wondered about it. That's why I did not mention the apparition at the court of the coroner."

She nodded towards Canon Louis.

"I was afraid that people would think me driven insane by the terror. And I could not explain how Michel appeared to me whole after the sound of his death-screams. If you had asked me for an explanation, sir, I just could not have answered."

Canon Louis twitched No, No, and looked worried.

"I see, but why bring it up now?" he asked.

"It preyed on my mind and I brooded on it," said Blanche. "I told only my friends and then Anne insisted that it could be an important clue to finding out who is the werewolf. So maybe I was not insane at the time?"

"Yes, it certainly could be a clue Blanche," said Anne. "If the Michel you saw was not really himself, then perhaps the Doloree who was seen at the time of the werewolf murder of Matilde may not have been the true Doloree."

Dr. Garzon looked worried.

"Still, it does not tell us the identity of the werewolf," he carefully pointed out.

"No, but if we know that the old nun is probably not the werewolf then we know to look for someone else without delay before another murder proves the point for us," added O'Neill with an air of urgency in his voice.

"That is my reason for telling what is so hard to explain," said Blanche. "More than anything I wish to bring the murderer of Michel to justice. I now feel sure that I saw the werewolf in disguise. There is no other real explanation. As you say Mr. O'Neill, what I saw could not have been

Michel. Why would he say that all was well when it was not? If it were his last farewell, a moment given by fate, a last window on life for his spirit to say goodbye, why would he try to lie? Why would he delude me? Why were there no tears in his eyes, no tender word of farewell? No, it was not my love only a demon that took on his appearance, surely his destroyer?"

"But you said that at first you thought it was his ghost," said Canon Louis. "Hmm. Yes, that's it. The apparition appeared after Michel's death. Therefore, it must have been his ghost. Yes, Yes."

He twitched, No, No.

Professor Vermillion and Dr. Garzon looked puzzled and uneasy.

Anne became tearful as she asked, "But why would his ghost be so untroubled after what happened?"

O'Neill was astounded and unable to control himself.

"Yes, why should Michel's ghost say that all was well after his body had just been torn apart by a werewolf. Also Canon Louis, why would a ghost be afraid of a gun?"

Canon Louis looked embarrassed, twitched, No, No, No and turned to Sergeant Antoine for an escape.

"Strange how you just happened to be there at the time, Sergeant Antoine. Hmm, self-confessed skeptic, perhaps into magic and Satanism?"

He scratched his chin.

"Very suspicious."

Then Canon Louis looked the sergeant up and down.

Sergeant Antoine was horrified.

"Me, Rev. Canon? Me? Oh, Reverend, I'm only exercising my democratic rights to be a mother-hater and a faith-denier. Motherhood and faith went out with the old world."

Then he straightened himself up and continued in a philosophical diatribe. "I'm a true revolutionary. You try making trouble for me and I swear, I swear I will provoke an international constitutional crisis. I stand on my secular rights against the foreigners. I'll appeal to the governor."

"Please be calm Antoine," whispered Anne, "we do not doubt your patriotism."

"Thank you Miss Anne," said the sergeant who now seemed to be relieved and appeased.

"Thank you my dear lady. I try to do my best to represent the people"

Then he saluted flamboyantly.

"No established church, no privileged classes, no land-owning establishment, no mother-love, no sentimentality. I try to be a true servant of the people. No firing squads, at least not without due process of law."

He saluted again.

"Firing squads and nooses - that is not the freedom."

Canon Louis continued to twitch, No, No and addressed the sergeant with an air of disgust.

"Yes, Yes, very patriotic Sergeant. Very egalitarian and fraternal and libertarian."

Dr. Garzon turned his attention back to Blanche who was still sitting quietly sobbing. He spoke to her in a kindly manner.

"Your story is very important my dear. It means that there is delusion and magic involved in these mysterious werewolf murders. It means that we must be very careful whom we blame. We cannot just blame anyone seen near the scene of the crime after what you have told us. I thank you for telling what must bring back very unhappy thoughts.

"But really the most unhappy thought of all is that the killer should be given his freedom to continue committing these revolting murders. Blanche it is important that you should explain your vision to the abbess soon and to Fr. Charles. For they also are concerned with justice in this parish."

"Both the Abbess Concordee and Fr. Charles control the great lands of the church," pointed out Blanche.

"So what, my child?" said Canon Louis. "There is nothing wrong with land ownership, is there?

"Oh no but it's just that I am so unimportant. I am afraid to visit them. Oh no, there is nothing wrong with owning land."

"Yes there is. It is immoral," said the sergeant.

"Maybe, but it's not yet illegal is it Sergeant?" said Canon Louis.

"Land needs to be more divided up to help more people," said Sergeant Antoine. "Too much big ownership means too much power for a few, which means too little freedom for the many."

"But you and I, Sergeant Antoine, are concerned with different aspects of the law," explained Canon Louis.

He twitched again.

"Isn't that so? The law not abstract radical ideas. No, the law, lay or clerical, but the law. Isn't that true Sergeant?"

The sergeant saluted.

"Canon Louis, the law, the whole law and nothing but the law."

Canon Louis twitched intermittently.

"Thank you Sergeant. Yes that's it, the law."

Anne looked at Blanche who continued to sit quietly.

"Well, maybe you could at least tell your story to Fr. Charles. He also can help innocent persons clear their name."

"I suppose I must talk to Fr. Charles. That's why I came here. It's just that I've been afraid. I'm not quite sure why. I fear that I suffered an illusion and people may think me insane or perhaps my story does contain some clue and, if so, the killer may try to kill me just to send people off the track of discovering his identity. I don't really see how my story could be helpful anymore now that you all know everything. For somehow I still feel afraid of telling my story. The truth is a terrible thing."

"No truer words were ever spoken, my dear Blanche," said Felix O'Neill. "The truth exposes not only persons but civilizations. Nothing is more dangerous than the truth. And many persons, for their own reasons, wish to suppress it, I think.

"Almost the whole of society at any given time is devoted wholly and single-mindedly to the sole and dedicated task of suppressing truth. That is what educational institutions and the press and literature and civilization and the law are all about. That is why they exist, to suppress the truth. Because the truth would set the people free and that would depose the establishment. So nothing on earth is as subversive or as revolutionary as the truth.

"Nevertheless, although what you have told us is just a very small part of the overall truth, we will take no chances. No doubt the werewolf wishes to suppress all clues, however small.

"We'll arrange a meeting at some quiet place for you to meet Fr. Charles. Why not in the church right here?"

Dr. Garzon put his arms protectfully around Blanche's shoulders.

"I will personally escort you back to the inn afterwards. That is a promise."

Blanche suddenly brightened.

"Very well Dr. Garzon. I trust you, so I'll talk to the priest."

"I think we have all made our contribution for now," said Anne. "Blanche, let us get back to the inn. I'm sure we are needed there."

Sergeant Antoine bowed to the two ladies as they headed back to the inn while the other members of the group remained deep in thought.

CHAPTER SIX

Blanche's Testimony Discussed

After Anne and Blanche had left to make their may back to the inn, the rest of the group began to discuss the merits of the full version of Michel's last moments.

"Well O'Neill, what do you think? What does it all prove?" asked Dr. Garzon.

"Blanche's story proves that the demon or werewolf was afraid of an old game-gun," replied Felix O'Neill. "It also proves that the werewolf is human and not a ghost. No, a mortal, one of us, perhaps you or perhaps me but certainly a mortal."

Canon Louis twitched negatively as he considered the new evidence.

"I don't see any great importance to this so-called new evidence. I take the point that the werewolf may, I say may, be able to adopt disguises and delude people but on the other hand illusions are well known to occur at the time of death."

"Yes Canon Louis," agreed Professor Vermillion, "but such death-bed illusions are usually seen by the dying person only and not by others."

"Yes Madame Vermillion, as you say, usually but not quite always. Occasionally others see and hear the banshee or beckoning ghost or whatever at the time of death."

"Such phenomenons are mere mass schizophrenia, Canon Louis, if you ask me."

"Be that as it may, Professor," insisted Canon Louis. "However, Doloree has made a full confession and signed it."

"Under fear and duress if you ask me, Canon," added Dr. Garzon. "Surely such a confession cannot be acceptable evidence."

"That will not be for me," said Canon Louis, "but for a secular tribunal to decide."

Felix O'Neill reminded the others that Doloree was attending a sickbed when Fr. Charles' mother was murdered.

"This can be proven by several reliable witnesses," he pointed out.

Canon Louis started to twitch again in his usual negative manner.

"We are going round in circles. It still remains to be seen whether the testimony of such witnesses holds up under the scrutiny of discipline."

Professor Vermillion was shocked by this comment.

"You don't mean that you intimidate the witnesses too?" she asked.

Sergeant Antoine confirmed that this had always been a very popular pastime of the establishment.

"That is what establishments are for - to protect the status quo with intimidation."

This comment made Canon Louis very angry.

"Sergeant, you are getting quite out of line again."

The sergeant saluted.

"Beg pardon, Rev. Canon, I withdraw the remark."

Then he scowled.

"But I still support the people."

"I think that Blanche's story proves that the werewolf is a master disguiser and could be anyone," said Mr. O'Neill. "Doloree is just a poor scared old woman whom the werewolf imitated to gain access to the priest's house."

Canon Louis agreed.

"We do not know who the true werewolf is at this time but the case of Doloree serves to strike fear into the hearts of the populace in general and therefore helps to suppress crime."

He twitched uncontrollably, No, No, and continued.

"It is a well established principle of law and order that it is a good thing to hang a few people now and then and indeed incarcerate as many as we can afford. Indeed, it is a public virtue to hang people regularly in order to terrorize the lower criminal elements."

Professor Vermillion was incredulous.

"My ears must be deceiving me. I don't believe this."

Felix O'Neill was also horrified at the canon's beliefs.

"But surely you hang only the guilty?" he asked.

Canon Louis raised his eyebrows as he considered this question for a minute and then started twitching once more.

"Well, human justice is imperfect. But yes, I agree with you, yes indeed, those whom we hang should preferably be guilty, yes indeed I would much prefer to execute only the guilty rather than the not guilty.

"Ah yes, my Christian conscience compels me to admit this. But while in an ideal world one would prefer to hang only the guilty, if the identity of the real villain is not known, well, we must hang somebody mustn't we? I mean we can't just ignore the crimes and hang no one. That would only encourage more crime, wouldn't it? Would you not agree?"

He looked around the group for a reaction.

Felix O'Neill took a deep breath at this statement in an attempt to control himself and then slowly and deliberately he voiced his thoughts.

"I think that the sooner we find and destroy the werewolf the better it will be for all the people living in these backward swamps and forests and waterways."

Canon Louis twitched negatively but Sergeant Antoine nodded and applauded his approval.

"Yes, yes, sir, Mr. O'Neill and don't worry, soon the people will abolish all hangings as mere tools of tyranny."

Canon Louis gave Sergeant Antoine a cold stare.

"I doubt it Sergeant Antoine. The ignorant masses just love hangings. Hangings and democracy are brothers. However, our hearing of the witness is over Sergeant. Let us go."

Canon Louis decided that he'd had enough discussion for now and murmured to the others that he had other pressing matters to attend to. So off he went back to the abbey.

Sergeant Antoine raised his hat and bowed to the others and followed after the canon.

"It becomes clear that this mystery is more complex, more intractable than we suspected," said Dr. Garzon. "What do you think O'Neill?"

Felix O'Neill thought for a moment and then carefully replied.

"I believe we have just received some valuable clues as to how the werewolf operates in almost supernaturally perfect disguises. But how? Or why? Or who?"

Professor Vermillion shook her head.

"We will have to sleep on it," she said. "But alas with our doors locked."

O'Neill concurred.

"And I would also advise keeping our windows barred, Professor Vermillion."

Dr. Garzon then suggested that they all meet again the next morning for a real scrutiny, a deep look at this delusional evil. He had some ideas of his own about the strange events but wanted to sleep on it before making his thoughts known.

Then the group departed and returned to their lodgings for the night.

After they had all gone from the graveyard, suddenly the apparent figure of Michel rose up from among the graveyard foliage and slowly beckoned with its left hand raised to about shoulder level. It's face was strangely expressionless and mysterious. Michel continued to signal with his hand as an evening mist began to descend and the daylight slowly faded on the old churchyard.

CHAPTER SEVEN

Suspicions

As arranged, Felix O'Neill, Professor Vermillion and Dr. Garzon gathered once again in the churchyard the following morning. This time they walked around and explored the overgrown foliage, tombstones and statues.

Dr. Garzon walked up and down a pathway lecturing animatedly to the others.

"I am just wondering what kind of a person uses magic spells. Perhaps an older man sells his soul to the devil in return for youth and strength and the feeling of well-being that comes with being thirty. At thirty anyone can conquer the world. But the devil cannot be kind or good or deliver on his promises. If he did, he would not be evil. By nature he is the Liar. So he stabs the older man in the back."

Felix O'Neill and Professor Vermillion were fascinated by Dr. Garzon's ideas. It was obvious that he had been thinking long and hard about the werewolf murders.

"The rejuvenator must obey the devil. In return, he must kill for the most cruel master in the universe. He takes upon himself, and is given by the evil one, the form of a wolf in order to kill and terrorize the innocent. He must recite spells and drink potions of the devil's choosing. He must also pay homage to the devil in ceremonies and finally, worst of all, surrender his soul to the devil forever. The devil's only purpose is to kill and to steal and to destroy."

O'Neill laughed incredulously as he slapped Dr. Garzon on the back.

Then with slight ironic humor he addressed his companion. "After that effort old chap you'll have the nerve to deny that you're a professional entertainer. What an imagination you have.

"You know your accounts of my cases are almost pure make-believe, especially where you credit me with the ability to time travel."

Professor Vermillion spoke up with an air of utter contempt.

"Magic. Hah. At least lycanthropy has been known for centuries to be a disease of freaks. And these steaming waterways and swamplands are just the sort of lab that freaks are born in. Look at the evidence of strange flowers and swamp creatures. Strange fish, crawlers, two-headed rats, weird-calling birds, worms, plants that squirm around and almost speak, horrible water-creatures. What genetic turmoil all around. Just the place for a person to be born naturally as a part-wolf - a wolf man, a cross between man and his most feared enemy - the ultimate genetic perversion - the sick man of nature, the freak, the werewolf."

Suddenly Sergeant Antoine arrived and greeted everyone. He raised his left hand in a gesture of despair and shook his head.

"My work is so difficult. I must arrest the innocent. It's just too easy to blame these horrible murders on some old ugly witch-like woman like my mother and she didn't do it I'm sure. So it would serve no purpose. Still, who cares about mothers? Ugh. No good."

"We know it," said Felix O'Neill, "but to all appearances, an old nun was seen at the presbytery when Matilde was murdered. That's one of the reasons why we believe that a shapeshifter is at work. The other reason was the testimony of Blanche the kitchenmaid."

"A shapeshifter? A what?" asked the sergeant. "Who or what is that?"

He was afraid and looked around suspiciously.

"We're still arguing about the how, the why and the who," replied O'Neill, "but one thing we are all mostly agreed on is that a shapeshifter is walking among us."

"A shapeshifter, Mr. O'Neill?"

Sergeant Antoine looked at the others as though begging them to deny it.

"Is this true?" he asked.

Dr. Garzon and the others nodded while Professor Vermillion was at a loss to deny it.

"It looks to be so," she said. "How it comes about exactly, nature or magic or secret science, those are the three big questions. As for the answer, we're not so sure but yes, a master disguiser is surely stalking these swamplands. We don't know who it is."

"But who could possibly be the villain?" asked Sergeant Antoine. "I mean the suspects?"

Then Dr. Garzon spoke to Antoine in an obvious serious tone.

"Anyone, Sergeant Antoine."

To illustrate his comment Dr. Garzon pointed at everyone present.

"You, me, him or her, anyone. The disguise is so good that we just cannot tell."

This caused Antoine to become very emotional and upset. He shouted at the others.

"But this is horrible. I hate it."

"None of us are above suspicion," said Professor Vermillion. "However, you Mr. O'Neill or you Dr. Garzon or I myself for that matter have just arrived and these murders have been going on for some time now."

Felix O'Neill shrugged.

"That means nothing. We could have been here before in disguise. Are we really whom we appear to be? Or perhaps the killings are the work of a murder club and one of us has just joined."

Sergeant Antoine pleaded with the others.

"Please find the shapeshifter, the werewolf. Every day that you delay, the powers that be grow stronger here. They will hang men and women just to entertain the poor, just to keep the poor happy and prevent a revolt. All the werewolf's victims have been poor. The poor always suffer. Why should the werewolf kill only the poor? Why should it support the powers that be? If you fail to catch the werewolf he will continue to kill. I fear for my life."

The others shrugged enigmatically while he continued in his tirade.

"I am a true believer in the common-wealth. I hate the politicians, churches, and landowners that have appropriated all the best land to themselves. I hate it all, from faith to flag. I have named the local tribunal a perverted form of law. As a true radical, I am a prime target of the powers that be. These powers may try to frame me for the werewolf murders or I may be its victim. We must capture it. But how to kill such a creature. Ah yes, I heard in the village that only a silver bullet can kill a werewolf."

Then he shrugged and spread out his hands in despair.

"Pure superstition I am afraid," said Felix O'Neill. "Perhaps someone somewhere tried to kill a werewolf with an old gun that aimed badly or weak buckshot or an old reused bullet. An old weapon would hardly kill a fierce werewolf full of the claw-strength of its super-charged life. The shot fails to kill; the creature lives to murder again. Then later someone succeeds with a silver bullet - a clean, hard missile. Lo, a superstition is born but I don't believe it for a second."

Professor Vermillion quickly removed her glasses and started to polish them intensely as she listened to another of Mr.

O'Neill's long dissertations. At the same time, Dr. Garzon blinked in astonishment as he tried to digest this lecture.

However, Felix O'Neill was undeterred and continued his monologue.

"My guess would be that any good and strong bullet from any solid gun would kill the werewolf. It is certainly afraid of guns in general. It is mortal not immortal; flesh not a ghost. Ghosts need no food.

"Supernatural monsters do not fear firearms. Still, no doubt its strength and surviving powers are formidable. It will be no pushover to trap or destroy this creature. Speed and strength will be needed as well as courage and cunning in order to match its prowess."

"It is said to be a crazy man who turns into a wolf at the full moon?" said Sergeant Antoine. "Zakotu, the villagers call him: an ancient one returned."

"My dear Sergeant Antoine," said Felix O'Neill, "whatever name the villagers have given this creature, it's not as simple as that, I think. No, it is not the usual madman, no ordinary lunatic but someone who has studied the occult. It is one who has acquired advanced powers, one who has learned and studied brilliantly how to rejuvenate, but not as a human, rather as a wolf of savage strength. It cannot turn back time, of course, to become truly young. Rather, the rejuvenation is linked to some borrowed animal power.

"Certainly such a person must be close to lunacy, as genius always is close to lunacy. In addition, the full moon does indeed affect the mind and passions to violence. It may play some small part. However, there is nothing like the myth, no sudden change to a wolf because of the moon, I do not think. Rather, I would say it is neither magic nor madness nor nature but the long-sought secret science of eternal youth - youth as expressed in the fierce blood of the werewolf."

Sergeant Antoine was awestruck by this information.

"Mr. O'Neill, you are a true genius. This is beyond my understanding. You had better tell our priest about all these strange sciences. Mind you, he holds to some old-fashioned religious beliefs but he is such a wise man in other ways."

Felix O'Neill was pleased at the simple flattery of being called a true genius.

"My dear Sergeant Antoine, Blanche the kitchenmaid has agreed to tell her story to the priest. She was afraid of being taunted as a criminal fool."

"I'll guarantee her safety from any such charge Mr. O'Neill," offered the sergeant, "if she'll just tell Fr. Charles. Also, I'll put a guard on her."

"But why a guard?" asked Dr. Garzon. "The holy cross will surely prove most efficacious against the magic of the werewolf."

O'Neill was irritated at this comment and raised his index finger at Garzon.

"My dear chap, please," said O'Neill. "The cross is only important to those who understand and believe in its significance. This proves only the humanness of the werewolf in general. How? A mere symbol would hardly cower Satan or any truly supernatural creature and there is no guarantee that this particular werewolf is superstitious. What Blanche needs is a gun not a cross."

"But against whom to protect her?" asked Sergeant Antoine. "All of us? See? So how does the werewolf disguise itself? How is the illusion done? How does it make us see it as someone else? Is it the evil eye?"

O'Neill nodded.

"Indeed, the eye is the alter animus - the other soul, perhaps the evil eye is part of the delusion. The evil eye is hypnotic and one should certainly avoid the hypnotic eye but hypnosis is probably only a small part, if any, of the delusion."

"Well if not hypnosis, what?" asked Professor Vermillion.

"Well Professor Vermillion, dear lady, this rational explanation is I believe the answer," responded Felix O'Neill. "Some very ordinary people in everyday life can disguise their voices and thoughts and faces to deceive others. For instance actors and spies. Why shouldn't some people be more advanced in secret sciences? Why should they not have a little more ability to deceive and disguise quickly? Why should they not have a more than ordinary knowledge of acting and illusion and hallucination?"

Professor Vermillion and Dr. Garzon glanced at each other and raised their eyebrows while Sergeant Antoine just looked completely lost. However, Felix O'Neill continued to elaborate on this theory.

"Most things in life are on a magnificent spectrum. People live from one to 120, people grow from three to nine feet tall and minds range from vegetable to genius. Therefore, why shouldn't some people be able to achieve a high level of disguisability as opposed to ordinary everyday deception?"

"But my dear O'Neill," asked Garzon,

"doesn't that level of disguise in speed and realism still break natural law? Isn't it tantamount to the magical?"

"Well old chap, according to our present knowledge of natural laws yes, I would agree. But my studies of the werewolf show that it can only enter into a home if invited. Although it is little bound by moral laws or psychological barriers. It is bound by bars and stone walls. A werewolf cannot read your mind or go through walls. Nor can it become invisible or foretell the future.

"If its disguises lie even partly in the perception of the inviters or hosts, is it not generally within the laws of nature? Sadly yes, horrors pile upon horrors as we study this monster of shape-changing in more detail and its advanced science of hide and go slaughter with impunity."

"So it is not content just to change into a wolf," added Sergeant Antoine, "it must masquerade as a friend to get close to its victim."

"I'm not sure that it does change into a wolf," responded Felix O'Neill, "rather, it changes into a human likeness."

Professor Vermillion was puzzled at this analysis.

"What do you mean exactly? I don't understand Mr. O'Neill. Surely its natural form is a human?"

"At first yes Professor but I suspect that there may be a secret biological potion that changes the fundamental structure of the body and makes it rejuvenated and strong and vigorous and very little subject to natural decay. Perhaps some secretion, some gland, some gene, some cell-changing essence taken from the bodies of strong animals like the wolf.

"Or in other cases, far out in the world, maybe the bear or the cat or the gorilla. So if the werewolf is a man or woman who has acquired the strength and prowess of a wolf it must look like one - smelly, hard muscles, fangs, ears for superhearing and so on. A human-wolf appearance will have become its usual and normal form. In fact, it may be a human that has come to look wolfish by its rejuvenation techniques."

Professor Vermillion appeared to be overwhelmed by this theory and shook her head in utter bewilderment as Felix O'Neill continued his diatribe.

"Of course the long hair, strong teeth and the wolf-like appearance are all really just superficial aspects. It is still human underneath, not a wolf. Perhaps a human laced with animal genes, who knows? Perhaps at the full moon the werewolf is a little weak and loses some of its power to deceive, if not its power to kill. Even with the help of its herbs or biological serum, it may lose the power to present itself as a normal human person. So at moments of great turmoil and passion such as the onset of the full moon, it loses its power to imitate someone else, its power to present a hallucination.

"At these few moments of weakness or mental distraction it appears as a wolf-man, its true changed and altered form as rejuvenated with wolf serum or genes or blood or whatever."

Dr. Garzon was absolutely stunned.

"Ah yes, that's well said O'Neill old chap, wolves in sheep's clothing not the reverse. You mean that it may become permanently a wolf-man and need an illusion to present the appearance of its former self or other harmless persons. Good heavens man, if this is true, then how many innocent people have been imitated by werewolves and then hanged for horrible murder and butchery that they did not commit?"

He shook his head in horror.

Then the sergeant asked in naïve astonishment, "You mean the werewolf was able to convince people that he was really someone else, some innocent person?"

"Yes indeed Sergeant Antoine," replied Professor Vermillion, "like the old nun Doloree who was suspected of killing Matilde."

Sergeant Antoine thought about this for a while, then remarked.

"What secrets it must have to be such a master of delusion and hallucination. What an argument against hanging, the tool of tyrants."

Dr. Garzon ruminated on this for a moment then asked Felix O'Neill.

"Indeed O'Neill, how do they do these things? Achieve this total illusion? This supernatural strength?"

"Garzon, my dear chap, we just do not know completely but if my studies have been on the right lines part of the answer is that the werewolf uses a combination of an electrical device. In fact, a belt and a special salve or ointment made from secret herbs that induce hallucination. The belt may be for emitting electrical strength to the werewolf and the herbs to cause illusion in the mind of the victims. You see, this is just an advanced form of natural chemistry operated by the werewolf. Again, when it is weak or distracted or sick or preoccupied with killing it is seen as a wolf-human, its true form if it is to enjoy the wolf's strength and terror."

"But Mr. O'Neill this is well beyond the frontiers of our known science," cried Professor Vermillion.

Dr. Garzon broke in at this point, "Indeed so my dear lady and it may well enter forbidden realms of mystical arts."

"Maybe so," said O'Neill, "but who is to say what is possible or forbidden?"

"Wouldn't you say, O'Neill, that these things should be limited by our natural conscience?" pointed out Dr. Garzon. "Who dares to understand the forbidden alchemy of the lost fountain of youth? Who would dare to experiment in these things, seeking to reverse nature? Such things are a revolution against the creator."

"Well, you do have a point Garzon," conceded Felix O'Neill. "But the werewolf has certainly achieved success in some advanced alchemy. Namely, it has achieved a mastery of the science of delusion - ways of appearing to change its identity almost instantly, almost perfectly. I can imagine a dedicated scholar researching the books and perhaps buying strange secrets and experiments. Finally, it finds an energy-emitting power source, some magnetically or electrically-operated and transferred animal power."

"But gentlemen," broke in Professor Vermillion, "I just can't believe that these things can be done by any type of science. In fact, no science or experiment or magic is necessary for this shapeshifting to take place.

"In fact Mr. O'Neill, you rightly said that all things are on a spectrum from high to low. Think about that for a moment."

Felix O'Neill smiled.

"I'm thinking dear lady. I rarely cease to think. So?"

"Well, all earthly creatures are related and we know that throwbacks are possible," suggested Professor Vermillion. "That's why there are people who look like apes, wolves, sheep, pigs, cows, elephants, tigers, dogs. Werewolfism is just that, but much more so. The werewolf is the pivotal type between man and wolf - a freak of nature.

"Science cannot cause the illusions that you claim. Science cannot produce a werewolf. A werewolf devours children and people and corpses. It howls in the graveyard for the carrion, digs up bones and graves with its bare hands. Can this be the result of science?"

"Ma'am," replied Felix O'Neill, "many a time has science gone to war or led the way to crime or created instruments of mass murder such as guns or bombs."

Dr. Garzon decided to agree with Professor Vermillion.

"Your theory is perhaps not quite scientific old chap. There are unanswered questions. For instance, who administers these illusory drugs to the victim of the werewolf or to the other witnesses of its delusion and why do people see these delusions?"

"Its obvious that the shapeshifter or werewolf administers the drug to the onlooker," replied O'Neill. "Don't you see the problem dear fellow - How?"

"Ah yes, O'Neill - How? At a distance? Without the victim realizing it?"

"Well let me see, my dear Garzon. Quite possibly by emitting a strange smell, sometimes noticed by the victim, sometimes not, just as ordinary smells come and go without obvious reason.

"If drugs taken internally through the mouth can cause delusions, why shouldn't strong smells also cause illusions? What is so odd about this? A faint smell of strange herbs has long been known and noticed and commented upon when a werewolf is near."

The others agreed that this might be possible.

"I'm only guessing," continued O'Neill, "but I think it is possible that this smell causes the victim to see things that are not there. No doubt there are other forces that contribute to the manipulation of the mind. Perhaps hypnosis, perhaps other strange and crafty arts of mental science such as telepathic rays that penetrate the brain."

Professor Vermillion gave out a gasp as Felix O'Neill and Dr. Garzon continued their analysis. She blinked and furiously cleaned her glasses and shook her head in disbelief.

"Well, you have made a good point, O'Neill. Hmm. It may be so. Who can tell?" said Dr. Garzon. "Even an apostle of the early church said, I'm quoting from memory now - No demons or wizards can change their true body or nature but some can alter their appearance to deceive. Some magic spell has been cast that causes the vision and other senses to be deluded. Reason is mocked and laughed at because the eyes see things that are not there and even the sense of touch is distorted to feel things that do not exist."

Then Felix O'Neill characterized their various takes on the whole mystery.

"You Professor Vermillion say it's all just a natural freak of evolution.

"And you Dr. Garzon believe it's magic and devious deals with the devil.

"On the other hand, I maintain it's all hidden secret science that one day will produce a talking beast that reads minds, that antichrist that will rule the world."

Professor Vermillion, exasperated with the others, interrupted with some sarcasm.

"I love this village Dr. Garzon. It's truly weird. You believe in magic and Mr. O'Neill believes in advanced science beyond the beyond. Fr. Charles hides. We have been expecting him too long even now. He agreed to meet Blanche but he hides."

Dr. Garzon responded defensively.

"Perhaps he's praying in secret. His mother has just been killed, you know."

But Professor Vermillion continued her tirade.

"There is the abbess who respects various interrogations the way homeopaths believe in remedies. The inhabitants of that abbey, the nuns, they're about as unique as snow in summer and average 90 years old. Pierre is strange and obsessed with his museum. Canon Louis believes in hanging not as a punishment for the guilty but as an act of public morale building and Sergeant Antoine hates his mother. I can't believe that that is compatible with the love of democracy and reform."

Sergeant Antoine had been sitting quietly nearby for some time listening to the debate. But when he heard the professor's comment about his mother, he just had to interrupt.

He laughed and bowed and then proudly strutted out his chest.

"Just so, ma'am. I do hate my mother and why not? All men must hate their mothers if they love democracy. Mothers are not democrats."

Professor Vermillion continued her outburst and ignored Sergeant Antoine.

"No one here is normal. Everyone is a freak. But especially you Mr. O'Neill. You are far too intellectual to be normal."

Felix O'Neill smiled.

"Of course, I forgot that women prefer men to be perhaps just slightly intellectual, clever but never quite clever enough to avoid manipulation and being outwitted by women."

The professor showed signs of disgust and then summarized her present thoughts.

"Anyone here could be the werewolf that is for sure."

"Except you Professor Vermillion. You are so normal, so very normal aren't you?"

"Are you sure Mr. O'Neill?" she replied.

"Oh yes Professor Vermillion, you and you alone are very suspiciously normal."

She shrugged, spread her hands then adjusted and cleaned her glasses.

"What of Anne the owner of the tavern - a very normal person also? I'm not the only one. Statistically, normal white sheep are bound to occur occasionally even among the monsters. I'm sorry, I'll try harder to be more freakish in future if only so as to feel more at home here," promised Professor Vermillion.

Dr. Garzon laughed heartily.

"Among us freakos – ho, ho."

Professor Vermillion blinked with some contrition. She polished her glasses again, shook her head, blinked and again adjusted her glasses.

"And as for you Dr. Garzon, your friend Mr. Felix O'Neill has thrown doubt on me because of my supposed normality, my suspicious normality. So you are the prime suspect according to your lifelong friend."

O'Neill was shocked.

"No, I never said so. That's not true"

"Yes you did Mr. O'Neill," insisted Professor Vermillion. "Yes you did. You said that even normality was suspect. So there it is."

CHAPTER EIGHT

Who is Who?

As the discussion proceeded, Anne arrived and joined the group. Sergeant Antoine raised his hat and bowed to her.

Professor Vermillion interrupted and wiped her glasses.

"Yes, yes indeed Mr. O'Neill, you have said and said repeatedly that advanced science is the tool of the werewolf. The werewolf is a super scientist, a master of science beyond the beyond. Possibly an older person you said trying to regain youth by means of werewolfism.

"No one, no one has greater knowledge of such things than Dr. Garzon, healtharian and homeopath from the internationally acclaimed School of Healthics. If science is the tool of rejuvenation then you may be the rejuvenated one.

"Come now who Dr. Garzon is better educated in the biological sciences and metaphysics than you, sir?"

Dr. Garzon was highly flattered and laughed in appreciation.

"And coming from a fellow scientist,

Professor Vermillion, that is a compliment indeed."

He smiled kindly at her.

"I can't deny that I know my fields of healthics and herbalism and homeopathy. Thank you, thank you, madam. However, I do not know my fields as well as a professor such as yourself."

"Well yes, maybe so, but I'm afraid that I'm not your werewolf," added the professor.

She blinked and wiped her glasses again.

"Indeed Dr. Garzon to quote the abbess and Canon Louis, do we just take your word for it? You are not the only well-educated suspect, of course.

"The canon is a lawyer and while lawyers are known for lying they are not in the least ignorant.

"The abbess is no doubt a very learned lady. She supervises an old abbey and museum that once dealt with witches and heretics. As such she must be a prima facie suspect.

"The priest is also very well versed in the theology of shapeshifting and illusion and knows all about deals with the devil. At the very least a priest has the knowledge to become a werewolf, if knowledge is indeed the key as you, Mr. O'Neill, insist.

"If, as I suspect, the cause of the terror is not magic or knowledge but nature perverted by these infernal swamps, then the least knowledgeable among us may well be the greatest suspects. If not knowledge then it is freak-nature as I suspect.

"An ordinary kind of person could just happen to be born a half-wolf. It could easily happen to any Tom or Dick or Harry. Anne maybe. Or perhaps it is Doloree. After all, she is certainly ordinary. Also, Doloree travels and so does the werewolf."

At this point she looked at Anne who in turn looked away guiltily.

"On the other hand, here we have just been found by Anne our hostess at the inn. Now Anne is also a very respectable and reasonable and helpful and ordinary person who could just conceivably have been born a werewolf."

Then naively, "Were you Anne?"

Anne was shocked and sat down on a tree trunk, stunned. She was comforted by Sergeant Antoine who was amused at Professor Vermillion's outburst.

The sergeant laughed.

"There, there, Anne. She's just been pointing the finger at everyone since before you joined us."

"Yes Sergeant you are right. Everyone is a question mark," remarked Felix O'Neill. "Is it possible Professor Vermillion that you have come here as an accuser, a cynic, not as a bona fide investigator?

"This throws suspicion upon your own motives. Are you a true scientific detective in search of knowledge? Are you trying to help or are you really just an agent of the killer? Or maybe you are the killer trying to deflect attention from herself?

"You have just thrown suspicion on everyone. That is a very, very odd function for a scientist who is supposed to use methodical inquiry. At the very least Professor Vermillion I can say that as a practitioner of objective inquiry you have failed totally."

"Thank you," returned the professor as she wiped her glasses once again.

"Yes I agree. I have failed so far because I just don't know who is the killer. You're right. The question remains, Who and what is the werewolf? I admit I am at a loss but I have tried."

Then everyone looked at each other with suspicion.

Felix O'Neill went into a quiet reflectful mood and then spoke up.

"Yes, so have we all, but. Who? Who?

Who? There's no point in accusing each other in this way. We have no proof of anyone's guilt. Why don't we just follow the clues? Then see who does what and sooner or later the finger of guilt will point at the person who is at the center of all the activity."

Anne looked all around and breathed a sigh of relief.

"Yes, why should we argue and accuse each other. The beautiful smell of winter flowers and evergreen herbs is in the air."

She looked up at the sky.

"Though the sky darkens somewhat."

Then Dr. Garzon breathed deeply.

"Yes, dry and remote but fresh and subtle. Surely it means an early Spring this year."

"There is Fr. Charles out on his rounds and visits," said Anne. "I must go out and ask him to join us. It is so important to get Fr. Charles on our side to help find the true shapeshifter. I am sure there is a great complexity to these horrible murders."

Sergeant Antoine kindly offered to escort Anne.

"Thank you Sergeant Antoine. You are so thoughtful," she said.

As Anne and the sergeant left together he bowed and raised his hat to the others.

CHAPTER NINE

Fr. Charles

After a short while Fr. Charles came into the churchyard. He was dressed in his long black outdoor robes and a cape. For some reason he was a little awkward and seemed not quite at home even in the churchyard.

Felix O'Neill looked at him suspiciously but greeted him respectfully. The others also greeted him warmly.

Dr. Garzon shook hands with Fr. Charles.

"You have suffered a terrible shock Father. All that we said at your mother's funeral holds true. If we can be of any help to you."

"Yes, if you need any assistance at the presbytery Fr. Charles," said Felix O'Neill, "I can send over any help you may need."

Fr. Charles interrupted, "Thank you, No. Everything is in order at the presbytery.

Professor Vermillion was tactful.

"We were looking out for you, Father Charles."

"I was visiting parishioners since early morning. Anne has just met with me and asked me to join you."

"Quite," said O'Neill. "It is just that we were worried that the werewolf murders are not being properly investigated. Sister Doloree the nun has been suspected because she or someone impersonating her was at the presbytery when your mother was killed."

"I'm sure it was Doloree," said Fr. Charles.

Felix O'Neill looked at him strangely, suspiciously.

"But Fr. Charles you said at the funeral that you caught only a glimpse of the person who visited your mother."

"Oh yes. Well, perhaps you're right."

He stroked his chin.

"Maybe I'm clutching after straws. Maybe I'm too anxious to find a culprit. Perhaps I'm a little suffering from shock."

O'Neill looked concerned.

"We know you've had a great shock but it is important to find the true killer. Blanche, the young kitchenmaid at the inn, has a story to tell you that seems to show that the werewolf is a cunning master of disguise and is probably not Doloree or Sergeant Antoine or anyone else seen near a murder.

"Can you speak to Blanche and see what you make of her story? See if you can elicit any clue to the killer's identity from your knowledge of all the people who live here.

"Neither Canon Louis nor the abbess will pay much heed to three strangers in town, however good our intentions.

"I will personally bring the girl to you Fr. Charles. I believe that her story is part of the proof that the werewolf is a shapeshifter throwing suspicion on innocent people by impersonating them at the time of these murders."

At this point the priest appeared shocked and confused. He licked his lips dryly and began to finger his rosary nervously.

"I see, a devilish impersonator. Good heavens."

"Father I would like to ask you about the werewolf," said Dr. Garzon. "As you know we're hunting it and hope to capture whatever it is soon."

"Yes?" replied Fr. Charles.

"When we catch it, the werewolf will not be easy to control," said Dr. Garzon. "What is the local feeling about how we handle it?"

"I don't quite understand. Could you be more specific?"

"Well Fr. Charles, can we dispense with a formal trial? Can we just catch it and kill it as a tool of the devil?"

Fr. Charles appeared uncomfortable as he considered the question.

"In theory yes. In ecclesiastical and civil law a werewolf, whatever it is, is not a Christian or a legal person but either a human follower of the devil or an animal. It is not murder to kill a werewolf.

"However, in practice no one person is fit to decide who is or who is not a werewolf or to carry out judgment against a supposed werewolf.

"Just as for any other crime, the accused werewolf is innocent until proven guilty and is entitled to a fair trial before being condemned to death. So the werewolf must be tried before a higher tribunal of judges, lay or clerical, according to the laws of this parish."

"I'm sorry Father but I'd be the last person to go along with that," said Dr. Garzon. "This is a strange parish indeed. If I see a werewolf all covered with hair and claws, I'm not going to wait for a jury to decide if it was a werewolf that killed me. I'll kill it, before it kills me, that's it."

The priest twitched his fingers and looked doubtful.

"I'll be happy to talk to your witness Blanche," he said.

Dr. Garzon nodded politely.

"Blanche, the kitchenmaid, you know her Fr. Charles but she is nervous and afraid to antagonize the werewolf."

"Yes, of course I know Blanche. She is a truthful girl in general and I'll be happy to hear her story and talk to her at full length about the matter. This would not be the best time or place. Send her to me in the church sometime tomorrow. I will try to help her or anyone else who may be involved."

Felix O'Neill interrupted.

"What you will hear from Blanche may change your mind about the guilt of Doloree or other possible suspects, such as Sergeant Antoine. I will bring Blanche to the church about 10:00 in the morning and take her home again. I will be well armed to protect her. She is such a frightened little girl that I feel it is my duty to protect her personally."

"Fine, Mr. O'Neill. That would be a good time. Ah, Dr. Garzon?"

"Yes?" said Dr. Garzon.

"My son, you surely didn't mean what you said about shooting on sight a mere suspect werewolf?"

"I was never more serious in my life," replied Dr. Garzon.

"I would worry about that," said the priest. "Please remember your position as a healer and not a destroyer. Also, it is best to leave it to the judicial system on principle and not to take the law into your own hands. Of course you have a right of self-defense in special cases."

Dr. Garzon was unrepentant but respectful and nodded perfunctorily.

"Yes of course, your reverence."

The priest smiled and counted his rosary beads but remained dignified although a little concerned as he departed.

After a while Anne returned and sat inconspicuously on a tree trunk.

"Mr. O'Neill surely Fr. Charles is acting strangely," she said. "He is perhaps a little mixed up but basically I have always thought him to be a straightforward and sincere and harmless person even though he has been thrown into turmoil by the horrible werewolf murders. Aye, like all of us in our different ways."

"Unless there is more to him than meets the eye, Anne," said Dr. Garzon. "Is he really just a simple priest? For that matter are you really just a simple innkeeper?"

Anne resented these comments and looked upset.

"I think so but I'm not sure. Are any of us what we appear to be? Or are we all something else in disguise? And I mean all of us. Are we what we appear to be or are we all demons masquerading as humans?"

Then Felix O'Neill interrupted curtly.

"Yes we're all demons. That reminds me Professor Vermillion of your outburst about this village and its freaks. You're right Anne, everyone is strange here. It's in the air like the smell of strange water creatures and crawling, mossy trees and herbs in wintertime. Of one thing I am sure, we are such a good democratic group here. I support popular super-science.

"You Garzon, my dear fellow, believe in magic for the millions.

"You Madame Vermillion believe that werewolfism can happen just by chance to anyone at birth, anyone at all - the werewolf of the people, by the people, for the people.

"And now we know that Fr. Charles advocates the constitutional due process rights of a vicious killer animal.

"Ah yes, all this is true democracy. No wonder the monster chose these far fields to tear and torment and eat human bones and perform its metamorphic homicide.

"A very good environment exists here for monsters and murder. I will say one thing for this little village it's certainly open to due process and democracy, especially the due process of decapitation and the democracy of death. And nothing is more democratic than death for in the end we all die, don't we Professor Vermillion?"

"Yes indeed Mr. O'Neill. I must agree with you at least on that point. Especially in this immediate vicinity," she added dryly.

CHAPTER TEN

The Priest in the Crypt

Sunken beneath the level of the church sanctuary was a crypt constructed of a severe gray-colored stone.

Inside the crypt were some pillars and many coffins. Several carvings of angels, crosses and other Christian symbols hung from the walls.

The church sanctuary was furnished with wooden pews placed neatly beside several huge pillars. There was also a large organ located at the extreme right of the sanctuary and hidden from the area of the crypt by two large pillars.

The sunken location of the crypt also removed it from the direct view of the organist. A mood of mysterious foreboding seemed to pervade the atmosphere.

Elene, the caretaker's daughter, set about lighting the candles in the sanctuary and when she had finished this task she decided to play the organ.

She moved some candles to the organ and then sat down to play some slow, eerie, traditional church music.

Felix O'Neill entered through the front of the church with Blanche who was frightened and on tiptoe. O'Neill reassured her with a relax gesture.

Blanche spoke timidly then raised her voice to a loud whisper.

"Fr. Charles I have come to see you as arranged."

There was only silence.

"Father are you there? Father are you there? Fr. Charles?"

Elene continued to play the strange and eerie music on the organ while Blanche continued to call out for Fr. Charles in a loud whisper.

"Is anyone there? You said you would meet me here."

Suddenly the priest in full frock quietly entered through the back door of the church. He walked through the crypt and mounted its steps so that his head and shoulders and waist were visible to Blanche. His movements were awkward and slow, creating a suspicion that he may not have been the real priest.

Felix O'Neill nodded to Blanche, smiled at her encouragingly and ushered her towards the priest. Then he left as he had entered through the front door of the church.

The priest beckoned to Blanche with his left hand raised to shoulder level to join him in the crypt. She hesitantly looked around the church and then slowly and quietly crossed the sanctuary and entered the crypt. The priest retreated to join her on the stone floor.

As Fr. Charles took Blanche's hand, his voice was kindly and reassuring.

"Blanche how nice to see you. Mr. O'Neill and Anne have asked me to talk to you about the apparition you saw at the time of Michel's death."

"I see that you have heard my story secondhand, Fr. Charles," said Blanche, "but I really need to find out if I have any important evidence that would be of help."

Then Fr. Charles reminded Blanche of his connection with the abbey.

"As an envoy of the abbess and the canon, it is my duty to interview witnesses and try to help them to assess if their evidence would be important in any trial."

"Well Father, I saw a vision of Michel beckoning to me after Michel was dead."

"No doubt a post-death apparition," said Fr. Charles. "I mean you just imagined it of course."

"No, it was a real apparition. I really saw it beckoning to me just the way that you did just now."

She stopped suddenly and put her hand to her mouth, suspecting that the priest was the werewolf.

Then Fr. Charles spoke to her with especially disarming friendliness, "Yes my child and did you see anything that might help you identify the werewolf?"

Blanche withdrew a pace and became hesitant.

"There was a swirl as of long skirts then the apparition was beckoning to me just the way you were beckoning to me a moment ago with your left hand."

In order to hold her attention, Fr. Charles developed a sudden urgent tone in his voice.

"So you and the others at the hotel think that the werewolf is a shapeshifter, a disguiser."

Blanche was scared and doubtful. She swallowed and nodded then slowly backed away.

"Yes Father."

Suddenly she ran behind a pillar followed by Fr. Charles who reappeared as the werewolf but still dressed in his priestly vestments. The werewolf seized her and began to strangle Blanche who was only partly visible behind the pillar. Blanche screamed.

Elene heard the screams above the sound of the music. She stopped playing the organ for a moment to listen but by then the werewolf's hands had closed around Blanche's throat and she had become silent. Elene continued to listen then shrugged and resumed playing the organ.

There was a struggle between the werewolf and Blanche. Blanche, half-dead, tried to escape as the werewolf continued to pursue her. She screamed again horribly just before she fell for the last time.

Elene again stopped playing and got up from the organ and looked around in fear. She put her hand to her mouth and peered into the dim corners of the sanctuary.

The werewolf, still wearing the priest's robes, ran to the stairs, mounted them and looked around for any witnesses. Then, seeing Elene, he crouched behind the pews and pillars to stalk her but she saw him and retreated. The werewolf sinisterly pursued Elene as she tried to hide from him.

Elene was terrified and knelt down to pray.

"Dear God in heaven protect me from this monster."

The werewolf heard Elene's voice and rushed towards her. Suddenly he became aware of a noise coming from outside the sanctuary. He looked through the church doorway and then hid behind a pillar.

Elene saw the werewolf and gave a suppressed scream. The werewolf slinked past her and away and made his escape from the sanctuary through the back door.

Elene was petrified and continued to scream loudly. After a brief hiatus, Felix O'Neill entered holding a gun.

He approached Elene.

"Elene you screamed, are you all right? Where is Blanche? A priest rushed past me just now with his head hidden in a cowl. Was it Fr. Charles?"

By this time Elene was shaking and trembling.

"It seemed to be both. Both priest and werewolf. Oh Mr. O'Neill it was terrible. The werewolf was crawling around here stalking me horribly just a few moments ago until I screamed and you came in."

They looked around the sanctuary and saw no one.

"It's gone Mr. O'Neill. I'm so glad it didn't attack you."

Then she called out.

"Blanche are you there? Are you all right?"

"I have a theory and a gun," said Felix O'Neill. "My gun is a large one and my theory is shoot on sight. I suspect that the werewolf is well informed and recognizes me as enemy number one. Most likely it saw me coming. It's crafty and skilled but it doesn't like guns. It's certainly not here now."

Felix O'Neill still remained concerned and agitated.

"But where is Blanche? Did you see her leave? I promised to return here to take her home after meeting with the priest."

Then he pointed to his gun.

"I drew this when I heard your screams. You haven't seen Blanche, have you?"

Elene remained sickly.

"No, but I heard screams coming from the crypt just a few minutes ago."

"Where's that?" asked Mr. O'Neill.

Elene walked towards the crypt.

"There, down those steps."

"Of course," said O'Neill, "that's where we saw the priest earlier."

When they entered the crypt they discovered the body of Blanche. Elene drew back in horror and began to weep bitterly. Felix O'Neill put his arms around her shoulders and sent her back up the steps. He looked closely at the body and then around the crypt. Grimly he still held the gun in one hand and moved it about slowly as he tried to focus on the werewolf.

He became sad and bitter, muttering to himself.

"So I sent you to your death, Blanche. How could I not have known? Hidden under another persona somewhere is a theatrical impersonator, cunning comedian and a liar who deceives and destroys his audience."

O'Neill continued to address the now lifeless body of Blanche.

"I'm sorry Blanche. I returned here too late. But I promise you one thing, I will kill your killer Blanche as soon as it clearly stands before me. No trial will ever take place. At least you have my word on that score."

Then with contempt in his voice, "I will send this shabby actor back to its motheaten wardrobe."

CHAPTER ELEVEN

The Priest in the Presbytery

It was twilight as Janice, the priest's housekeeper, sat quietly knitting in the dimly lit presbytery. Organ music could be heard playing in the distance.

A tone of regret for the deaths of Matilde and Blanche seemed to pervade the atmosphere. There was also a mysterious and sinister, fear-laden element as the question of the werewolf's identity became the obsession of everyone in the village.

A misty pall hung over the nearby gravestones and over the cypresses and weeping willows and bushes scattered among the graves.

Two guards carried the body of dead Blanche on a stretcher. They were followed by Mr. O'Neill and Dr. Garzon who held Elene by the shoulders to comfort her. The group paused near the side of the presbytery and Elene stood sobbing.

The well-barred front door opened and Elene's mother Janice came out past the barred window which overlooked part of the graveyard.

She looked at the body and asked, "Elene what is it? Who is this?"

"Oh mother, this is Blanche the kitchenmaid at the inn. She has been killed by the werewolf in the crypt."

"No," cried Janice, "surely a werewolf, a monster, cannot kill a Christian in a church? If this can happen no one can be safe anywhere."

"I'm afraid so mother. I saw the werewolf dressed like a priest. It stalked me in the church and ran off only when I screamed and it saw Mr. O'Neill coming with a gun."

Janice shook her head and sobbed.

"These days we've seen so much of death. Please bring the remains into the presbytery. She can rest there until the burial."

As the organ music continued to play, the guards slowly lifted the stretcher again.

Fr. Charles entered the graveyard. He was upset and a little distraught as he buttoned the collar of his cassock but his manner remained calm and friendly and sympathetic.

"What is this? What is going on here?" he asked.

"It's Blanche from the tavern," replied Janice. "She's, she's the latest victim of the werewolf, Father."

Fr. Charles shook his head in dismay. Then calmly and with visible self-control he asked, "Surely this werewolf nightmare must end soon?"

He knelt and briefly prayed in silence over the body of Blanche and then stood up solemnly and ordered the guards to take the body into the parlor.

The guards slowly carried Blanche along the side of the house, past the window and through the front door and on into the parlor. Elene and her mother sadly watched the body being moved.

Suddenly Canon Louis arrived and joined the other mourners.

Felix O'Neill queried the priest as though probing for a reaction.

"Fr. Charles, Blanche was killed in the crypt."

Fr. Charles seemed upset.

"First the presbytery and now the crypt. This murderer has no reverence for either life or sanctity."

He shook his head.

"However, now I must go to the church to hold late night prayers."

Felix O'Neill then asked the priest

delicately, "Fr. Charles, I haven't forgotten that your mother was a victim and I'm sure you must be upset but didn't you remember that you had, only yesterday morning, agreed to talk to Blanche in church. That was why she was there."

Fr. Charles looked puzzled.

At this point Canon Louis spoke up.

"Yes Father, you were the one who was supposed to meet Blanche in the crypt so I hear."

Fr. Charles stiffened slightly at the sight of Canon Louis and answered him firmly and slowly.

"No, Canon Louis, you are mistaken. I made no such arrangement. I have been praying greatly about these werewolf murders over the past few days and therefore I have been somewhat secluded. I have made no special arrangements to meet anyone. Of course, I have spoken to a few parishioners as they have visited me and I have conducted prayers in church at the usual times."

Canon Louis looked at Felix O'Neill in astonishment.

"Mr. O'Neill surely this is not what I have heard. Did you not arrange . . .?"

Janice suddenly interrupted.

"Fr. Charles has not been away from

the presbytery today and very little, only as far as the church, during the past few days."

Felix O'Neill became interested and puzzled at this.

"Janice, at 11:00 a.m. this morning?"

"Yes Mr. O'Neill. Fr. Charles was here in the presbytery at that time. A parishioner called to see him and I introduced the caller to the Father just about eleven."

"Janice, are you sure?" asked Canon Louis. "Can you swear to it?"

"Absolutely. I can swear to it. I could hear him praying here in the presbytery most of the morning."

Janice felt that she had to justify his strange behavior.

"It is understandable. Matilde suffered a most terrible death only two days ago. And this whole area is terrorized by a killer werewolf. We all need prayer."

Felix O'Neill was sympathetic.

"Yes of course, it's understandable and I believe you absolutely. This confirms my belief that the werewolf is a masquerader of genius. He had the gall to visit us in the churchyard yesterday morning posing as you, Fr. Charles. Then we unwittingly arranged a meeting between Blanche and this false priest who was the werewolf."

Felix O'Neill continued with bitterness in his voice, "Without knowing it, we put her into the hands of her destroyer. How could we have been so deluded? How could the werewolf have duped us so completely? It could have been an illusion caused by the smell of delicate herbs that hit us just before the false priest appeared.

"I admit that I was suspicious of the false priest yesterday morning but I thought his strangeness was understandable and natural in view of the recent tragic murder of his mother."

Canon Louis started to twitch again.

"You were suspicious Mr. O'Neill but you did not report your suspicions to the authorities?"

Dr. Garzon had been quietly listening to the conversation and suddenly spoke up in defense of Felix O'Neill.

"Ah yes, to the authorities. The authorities like you Canon Louis. That reminds me Canon Louis, you are always close at hand when any werewolf activity takes place. Sometimes the priest is here; sometimes the abbess, so we have heard; sometimes the sergeant or Pierre the curator; sometimes one or two of the ancient, the demented, the religious sisters. Yes, even sometimes Mr. O'Neill or myself are nearby.   But you are absolutely never far away from homicide, are you Canon?"

These comments made Canon Louis nervously twitch, No, No.

"It is my duty to be close to the people. Do you have any proof against me?"

"No, nor do you have proof against me or the abbess or Anne or Pierre or Sergeant Antoine or Mr. O'Neill or anyone else for that matter.   That is my point," responded Dr. Garzon.   "We are all suspects."

"Yes indeed, including you yourself Dr. Garzon," said Canon Louis twitching. "You admit that the werewolf stood among you yesterday morning and you did not see or at least did not report anything suspicious. Surely this disguise did not fool all of you? Who all was there?"

"Anne, Sergeant Antoine and let's see," said Dr. Garzon.

Suddenly Felix O'Neill interrupted.

"No my dear Garzon, Anne and the sergeant had left the churchyard when the priest met us."

"You're right O'Neill," said Dr. Garzon.

"So there were just you Garzon and I and Professor Vermillion. Just we three."

"You're absolutely right, O'Neill."

Then Dr. Garzon brightened up.

"Right, I have it.   Canon Louis there

are witnesses that O'Neill and I were both in the same place at the same time as the false priest, the werewolf."

Dr. Garzon became triumphant and full of some satisfaction.

"Therefore, that is proof that neither O'Neill nor I nor Madame Vermillion is the shapeshifter."

But Felix O'Neill responded sadly.

"I'm afraid it's not as simple as that, dear fellow. Is it Canon Louis?"

Canon Louis twitched enthusiastically.

"That's right Mr. O'Neill. Already we are considering the possibility that there is more than one werewolf. And as for who was or was not here, that is a matter of your word only and you might be in collusion."

Dr. Garzon thought about this for a minute.

"Yes indeed, I see what you mean. And of course we know so little of the magic of shapeshifting. It does seem unlikely but it might even be possible that the werewolf is able to project his delusion as some kind of astral image so that one of us is the shapeshifter deceiving the others, even as we stand around listening to the living ghost. But we are, in effect, looking at the projected alter ego of the werewolf. We just don't know how much power has been given by the evil one to these shapeshifters."

Janice was horrified.

"So the werewolf has stood among us disguised as a priest and we do not even know who or what it was?"

"It looks that way Janice," said Felix O'Neill with a sympathetic tone in his voice. "But everything is illusion and delusion at this wretched moment."

Elene was puzzled.

"Can't anyone recognize him? Surely no disguise could be perfect?"

"Ma'am," said Dr. Garzon, "I suspect that this shapeshifting is simply magic, plain, old-fashioned, deals-with-the-devil, potions, spells and magic. That's why the werewolf is still on the loose."

Then Felix O'Neill placed his arm comfortingly around Elene's shoulders.

"Nevertheless, I think Elene has a good point. The werewolf is human. It fled from me earlier because I was armed. Also, why would it show itself to us just to get close to Blanche to destroy her unless it feared that she could identify it? Perhaps its disguise may have slipped a little when it killed Blanche's boyfriend - Michel.

"Perhaps the werewolf was trying to test Blanche to see if she could remember anything incriminating.

"Maybe it feared that she could recall some detail or identify the sinister herbal smell of mind-madness and illusion, just anything that would help to identify the werewolf.

"It's hard to see why else it would go after one single victim like that. Yes, all this indicates a fear of being identified. This could only be due to a possible chink in its armor of shapeshifting.

"No, it's not anywhere near infallible magic. It is all the work of man."

Elene and Janice were cheered a little by Mr. O'Neill's encouragement.

Then Fr. Charles addressed the others carefully and with concern.

"I just can't believe that this creature had the skill and effrontery to impersonate me. It's terrifying to think of shapeshifting. My double from the lower regions of fear. This creature is a deceiver and a fugitive from truth. Its spirit floats over us all like the misty pall above the waterways. It floats around these sullen tombstones. It laughs and gloats over us, mocking us with its cries of who or what am I? Where am I? It sticks its thumbs in its ears and waggles its fingers at us; it puts out its tongue at us as it plays its lewd and childish game of hide and go slaughter."

Janice and Elene looked around in fear and held hands.

Felix O'Neill rubbed his chin thoughtfully as he listened to the priest. Then he tried to comfort the others.

"You two dear ladies be sure to lock and bar all doors and windows. Now go inside and rest. This has been a long and sad morning for all of us."

The presbytery was still dimly lit as Elene and her mother Janice slowly and sadly entered through the front door and into the parlor. They decided to sit quietly beside the body of Blanche.

CHAPTER TWELVE
The Werewolf Debate

Canon Louis twitched.

"While any one of us standing here now could be the werewolf, yet the main suspect has confessed. As well as Blanche, I have to inform you that in the past few days there have been at least three other killings in the area.

"Also, it's very suspicious how the suspect Doloree and two other suspects have gone missing again quite suddenly. There may be more than one werewolf, you know."

Dr. Garzon quickly interrupted.

"Canon, you surely must realize that anyone would confess to anything in that old abbey with its memories and the museum of the inquisition."

Canon Louis responded coldly and calmly.

"Perhaps you are right, Dr. Garzon. Who knows? But Pierre the curator is no inquisitor. Some of Doloree's sister nuns maybe believe that confession is good for the soul. I admit that.

"But, of course, you don't think the old machines are still working. No, they were banned by our bishops centuries ago. Why, it's just a museum. It's all a bluff to get at the truth. It's all just atmosphere with a few silly old eccentrics to add realism."

"You mean with a few raving lunatics thrown in for terror," added Felix O'Neill, sarcastically.

"By the way, who are the other two missing so-called suspects?"

"Professor Vermillion and Antoine the sergeant," replied Canon Louis.

O'Neill gave Garzon a look of shock.

"Professor Vermillion. Of course, we haven't seen her all day and Antoine did tell us that he himself was a suspect."

Dr. Garzon quickly interrupted Felix O'Neill.

"Yes, Madame Vermillion said she was going to investigate the abbey grounds for clues."

Canon Louis nodded in agreement.

"Indeed, she was seen prowling around the abbey. Sergeant Antoine was guarding her at the time before they both went missing."

"Surely Canon, all these confessions and disappearances cannot be right when the werewolf is still at large?" said Felix O'Neill.

"Well I admit I'm beginning to doubt that there could be so many werewolves," replied Canon Louis. "I will go now to the abbey and discuss this with the abbess and I would value your insights. Perhaps Fr. Charles will also help."

"Certainly Canon Louis, I will join you in the abbey in a little while after vespers. I too doubt the wisdom of all these suspicions and even one inquisitional confession. It's all downright primitive in these modern times."

Canon Louis nodded and bowed to the others then made his way towards the abbey.

Faint and sinister organ music from the church continued to float over the graveyard.

"It is almost time for vespers," said Fr. Charles. "I must go to prepare for evening prayers."

"Father, one thing before you go," said Dr. Garzon. "Madame Vermillion is a bona fide natural scientist and pathologist. Will you help us to find her?"

"Yes Fr. Charles," added Felix O'Neill, "Professor Vermillion has become somewhat of a colleague to Dr. Garzon and myself. Do please help us find the professor as well as Sergeant Antoine and Sister Doloree."

"Certainly gentlemen. Of course Mr. O'Neill. I'll meet with you both along with the abbess and Canon Louis later at the abbey."

He smiled as he commented.

"As one of judicious outlook, it's my duty to throw the net wide enough to catch all possible fish, of course."

Then he clasped his hands together and bowed to the others as he departed through the presbytery front door.

However, Felix O'Neill noticed a very strange smell.

"Once again I smell that herbal smell faintly coming and going," remarked O'Neill, as he sniffed the air. "This is a strange and horrible place. Are we also going to go missing? I don't trust these people. There's something vile in the air. I'm glad we came here, my dear chap. I wouldn't have missed this mystery of murders, lies, duplicity and disappearances for the world."

Dr. Garzon disagreed.

"I was educated in a large city. I didn't need to come to these forsaken swamps to see decadence and horror."

O'Neill tried to encourage Garzon.

"Cheer up old friend, this experience is

just right for your next novel of mystery and the supernatural. Also, I'm speaking of my personal preferences for real life adventure."

"Oh yes, I see what you mean," agreed Dr. Garzon. "But I must say that I've found little here to entertain me or to help me find out about the mysteries of life. Indeed, it is all most confusing to me so far.

"It particularly disturbs me that the werewolf has been flourishing as never before since we arrived here. Perhaps our coming has challenged it or maybe it feels that, like the devil, its days are short and so it runs back and forth seeking whom it may devour.

"In some strange way the danger of our presence has inspired and invigorated it and sent it into a frenzy of killing like a child joyfully devouring all at a birthday party. Perhaps all this masquerading and killing is an insult to us, to discredit us, so that the authorities will ask us to withdraw? Or perhaps involuntarily one of us is the werewolf.

"Earlier, it seemed that the werewolf was only occasionally able to be here. But now it's here all the time. The thing that may be one of us stalks and strikes."

O'Neill and Garzon looked at each other with some suspicion.

"I agree with your questions my dear Garzon," said O'Neill. "Is everything what it seems to be? A madhouse? Or is there method in all the madness?

"Anyway, people will be locked and barred in their houses tonight, looking out of their windows suspecting their neighbor, peering out over the far waterlands and swamps. The tavern will empty all at once as people go home in groups, with crosses and guns with silver bullets. But will it help them?"

Felix O'Neill shook his head.

"Indeed O'Neill, we just don't know how much power and magic the werewolf has," wondered Garzon. "What if it has a second self? A second self, an alter ego, an astral projection. Then it could appear to be out there but really be right here. Right with us as we leave on the dark-weeded road to the abbey. Each of us will be wondering are you, am I, the werewolf? Who or what is the werewolf?"

O'Neill shook his head and looked at Dr. Garzon strangely with utter incredulity at his idea.

"A second self indeed. Consciously or subconsciously in existence? Oh never mind. Let's go."

As O'Neill and Garzon started to walk towards the abbey there was silence, apart from the church organ music which seemed to get a little louder as the wind had changed direction. The daylight drew to a close and the stars flickered.

After a little while the werewolf, still dressed as a priest, came out from behind a tombstone and gloated and howled and ate and laughed and threw bones and earth and stones around. Its claws tore at the graves, their pebbles and soil and threw the grass and flowers wildly about.

CHAPTER THIRTEEN
Fears and Pleadings

At the same time as the darkness began to fall, candles were being lit inside the home of Janice and Elene.

The mood was eerie as Janice lit the candles and Elene played a slow dirge on the organ.

The body of Blanche still lay covered by a sheet on a table.

Janice's manner was homely and wistful as she interrupted Elene's organ playing. But it was obvious that she was fearful when she spoke to Elene.

"This house is not the same. I've never known this home to be so eerie. It's strange Elene but I've been the housekeeper here for twenty years since your father died. Always when there was a dead body resting there, I felt somehow that was that. In other words, that was the end of that person's life. Someone had died and there was no more to be said.

"But now that this poor dear child was killed, by heaven knows what or whom, it's as though she is lying there accusing us all. For we are all suspects. It's as though this is just the middle of a long, sad story and not the end."

Elene, who had been playing gently on the organ while her mother had been speaking, leaned back and looked towards Janice.

"Yes mother, I know. It's like there's a question hanging over her like the misty pall hanging over the graves. She seems to be saying, Who? Who or what? Find it and stop it right away. Whatever it is. It killed Michel and impersonated him and now it has killed me. Whom will it impersonate next? Who will be next to die?"

Janice, with a worried expression on her face, nodded in agreement.

Then Fr. Charles appeared to come from the direction of the church. He was dressed in outdoor black clerical vestments.

"Janice and Elene, I have to go to see the abbess now that vespers are over. Disappearances, strange goings on in the old museum of confessions. I may be late in returning. Be careful whom you let in. I'm sorry I can't be here with you."

"We know there is a shapeshifter out there," said Elene. "The monster that I saw in the church was not you Fr. Charles. And it was not Doloree who visited us the other night. I'm sure of that too."

Janice pleaded with Fr. Charles.

"O please Fr. Charles, don't leave us tonight. I was just saying . . ."

She suddenly looked towards the body of Blanche.

"I was just saying that things are not the same here as they have been in the past. We'd be so afraid here on our own."

Fr. Charles answered Janice in a gentle manner.

"I understand but that's why I need to see the canon and the abbess. It's my duty to try to sort things out with them. I'm afraid that innocent people are being set up as suspects and perhaps even tortured into confessing murders that they did not commit.

"Also, I myself have been impersonated and therefore I am a prime suspect. This is something I just can't leave until tomorrow. I need to help the innocent suspects tonight. Perhaps I've been spiritually self-indulgent in shutting myself up and giving way to prayer these past few days.

"Janice it really seems to me that these werewolf murders have thrown all of us into chaos, including me and also the canon and the abbess.

"Indeed our whole law and order process is crumbling into chaos. There is even a suspicion that the rusty skeletal museum of inquisitional days may have been brought back into use. Everything is falling apart. Anyone could be the werewolf. It's all a horror of blood-games and mind manipulation. We need to get together with each other and try to reason it all out. I'll be back as soon as I can."

Janice thanked Fr. Charles.

Then Elene started to plead with him.

"Father, please don't leave us alone for too long."

He understood their fear and tried to give them words of comfort as he made the sign of the cross.

"I'll try not to. God bless both of you."

Then he asked Janice to keep the candles burning in the church for a little while longer.

"It's still early for those who seek an evening prayer for many of the village folk are nervous these days."

Janice nodded.

Elene pleaded with him to be careful on the road. Then both Elene and Janice stood up and made the sign of the cross in a reluctant gesture of goodbye to Fr. Charles as he left through the barred door and walked towards the castle.

After he had gone Janice barred the door again behind the priest. Distraught and on the point of tears she buried her head in her hands.

Elene sadly bowed her head over the organ and started to slowly play a sad but strange tune. Then she rose from the organ and stared for several seconds at the covered corpse of Blanche.

Janice became fearful.

"I wish I didn't have to go out tonight but it's my duty as housekeeper to keep the later lights burning in the church."

Elene agreed and became subdued.

"This is a night for bolted doors and windows."

Then she went to the front window and looked out and waved her left hand.

"Trees, bushes, the crawling, smelly swamplands and over here tombstones. Anything could be hiding out there. It's just not right that you should have to go out on a night like this."

Then suddenly she turned around and pleaded with Janice.

"Mother, I'll go instead. I'm better able to scream or fight or run or hide than you are, my dear."

Janice shook her head and smiled uneasily.

"Don't be silly, I've been doing this candle lighting at night for years and years and it's second nature to me."

Janice embraced Elene and kissed her reassuringly.

"I promise to be careful and besides I can scream or hide as well as anyone. Maybe not run or fight but scream and hide. Yes, if I see anything, anything walking towards me."

She suddenly broke down, sobbed, knelt down and prayed silently.

"But mother there is no one out there wanting to pray in the church. They're too afraid. They are praying at home instead."

"No wonder," said Janice. "Oh, I'm so afraid to go out."

Elene picked Janice up and set her in a chair.

"Mother, of course you don't need to go out. Your housekeeping duties end when there is something deadly and strange out there. I'll go instead if the church's work really must be done."

Janice shook her head and composed herself somewhat.

"No, No, Elene. You would think that a woman could do a simple thing like go to church without being afraid. What kind of world are we living in? It seems like only a little while ago that you and I were so happy."

She spread her hands in a gesture of hopelessness and despair.

"I had the best job in the village as the priest's housekeeper and I had respect and friends and you as my devoted assistant. Then all at once everything seemed to crumble away like a broken riverbank and we have fallen into a fen of bones and blood.

"Why did these werewolf killings come so close to home, when home is the church, the presbytery? Suddenly for no reason life becomes a vase that falls from your hands and smashes at your feet."

Elene shook her head in despair.

"Maybe that is why the werewolf sees this church and the Father and his household, the parishioners and believers, as the enemy. An enemy to be destroyed. The fishermen of the waterlands rumor that the werewolf is Zakotu - an old spirit of the waterlands come alive to drive out the latecomer and the Christian."

"Then we are prime targets," said Janice, "for we are right in the center of the latecomer's religion."

Unseen by Janice or Elene, a hairy-clawed hand, as of a werewolf kneeling down, suddenly appeared outside the barred door and tried to find a way into the house. Then it disappeared for a moment. Seconds later, the hairy claw appeared again and tried the handle of the door and pushed and groped across the lower part of the barred glass panel on the door. The door rattled as the claw disappeared once more.

Elene started to shiver. "It's cold out in the churchyard. It's still winter. Just don't go out tonight. Listen."

She got up and sat at the organ again and played a spiritually inspiring but still a slow and nostalgic tune. Then she paused and smiled at Janice.

Janice smiled back tearfully.

"Yes, that old song reminds me of the days when life was better. When did it all change? No new person has come to live here. How Elene? Of course, the three newcomers who investigate."

"I don't know, mother. Mr. O'Neill the detective says he has researched about werewolfism and it has to do with someone growing old."

"But we're all growing old Elene."

"Yes I suppose so but maybe someone

finds that it just suddenly hits them and they need to grow younger again."

Janice nodded. "So they use spells and get into forbidden arts."

Elene started to shiver again.

"Perhaps. I just don't understand."

Janice finally decided that she had to go and do her duties at the church.

"Well, it's my job to light up the candles in the church. I can't ask you or anyone else to do it. I'll have to go out. I should have more faith. How can I take all the respect that goes with being the clergyman's housekeeper and still behave like an unbeliever?"

"Mother please, everyone who's been killed so far has been a believer. Faith has nothing to do with it."

"Well, if not faith then fate. I must do my job Elene."

Elene cried out, "Mother, please don't leave me."

Then, as one acting quickly, suddenly in a great hurry, to overrule a change of mind, Janice wrapped a light shawl around her head and shoulders and with swift determination left through the front door, closing it firmly behind her. Her footsteps echoed very quickly into the distance as she disappeared from sight.

CHAPTER FOURTEEN

The Werewolf Returns

After Janice had disappeared into the distance, Elene ran in fear to bolt the front door.

Almost at once an image of her mother showed its face at the door and knocked. Elene, seeing her through the barred glass, rushed to open the door. The false mother entered quickly and breathed deeply as the door closed. She held her heart as one in a state of fear and shock. At this point it was not clear to Elene that this mother Janice was an impostor.

"Oh my heart. My heart."

She covered her eyes with her hands.

"No, No. I just can't believe it. I can't believe what I saw out there."

She looked at Elene strangely with a hint of cunning and a piercing stare that said, Do you believe me?

"Mother what did you see?"

False Janice looked away.

"I cannot tell you. No. No. No. I am afraid that I am going insane."

"What? Please mother, you must tell me what you saw."

"I saw someone waiting for me among the tombs."

"Who?"

False Janice shook her head.

"No, No. It can't be," she cried out.

"Mother, I need to know for my own safety."

"Yes, I know that's true but I must be mistaken. I am suffering from delusions."

She paused and pointed to the body of Blanche.

"It was her. It was Blanche. I saw her out there waiting by the graves."

Elene was horrified.

"If that was her out there then who is this in here underneath that shroud there?"

False Janice pretended to be terrified.

"I don't know. Perhaps it wasn't really Blanche out there. No, perhaps it was it."

"The werewolf?" gasped Elene.

"Yes, the shapeshifter or werewolf or whatever it is."

"But how can it just masquerade as almost anyone with such contempt for truth? Who or what is it really?"

Elene wondered at this and feelings of confusion clouded her mind.

"Mother, surely the werewolf can't be Blanche?"

Elene looked towards the corpse lying on the table.

"Oh Blanche, please be at rest. Please do not come back to seek revenge. Do not be restless and do not blame us for not knowing that you were in danger. Blanche please sleep. Please sleep on and do not walk among us anymore."

False Janice looked satisfied, even mildly pleased, at this invocation of Blanche by Elene.

"Yes Elene, I too pray that Blanche will rest in peace and be still."

With their backs to the door, they both looked at the corpse.

Suddenly there came the sound of a finger tapping at the door. It was the real Janice standing outside the barred door with her face pressed against the glass.

Outside and looking in, the real Janice was amazed that Elene would not open the door for her. So she pointed to the false Janice's back and grimaced questioningly at Elene, as if to say, Who is that?

The false Janice hid her face from the real Janice.

Elene saw the real Janice looking in at the window and clutched her mouth in fear.

She looked from one to the other.

She spoke to the false Janice.

"Oh mother look at the figure outside."

Then she shouted to the image that was standing outside, "You are not my mother and I will not let you in."

The false Janice pretended to be terrified and did not turn but kept her face hidden from the real Janice who stood outside.

"It's it. Don't let that thing in. It's the werewolf, the shapeshifter. Play the organ again. Play something spiritual and good to drive it off."

Elene sat down quickly at the organ and began to play badly and with many mistakes a spiritual but sad melody. Her fingers stumbled.

The real mother outside continued to gesticulate and grimace and point to the false mother inside.

The false Janice kept her head covered with a shawl and sternly and consistently turned away from the door.

Outside, the real mother was confused and moved a little way off and became no longer visible at the door.

Elene's back was turned and she did not see this incident. She continued to play the organ badly.

The false mother doubly locked the door, driving home an extra bolt. Then she clawed the air and approached Elene threateningly from behind.

"Let's keep it out Elene. It has run away since you started playing. I'll keep a lookout."

Elene looked over her shoulder as the false Janice stopped clawing the air.

"Yes mother, please do."

False Janice once again approached Elene from behind and looked at her as at a target.

"Elene I think the werewolf has gone now. Just keep playing hymns."

As she said this, she coughed and choked on the words.

Elene played louder in panic and then stopped suddenly. She stood up and turned to see false Janice threatening her. Then she ran across the room and faced the false Janice whose back was to the door.

Her real mother suddenly appeared outside again and grimaced and clawed viciously at the window. She moaned and cried faintly in despair so as to create some doubt as to who was Elene's real mother.

The imposter hid her face from the door and window by drawing her shawl around her head as in fear.

Elene looked in horror at her real mother outside.

"Do not be afraid daughter," said the imposter. "The bars are reinforced and it cannot break in because it is bound by physical laws. It must break in, which is impossible, or be invited inside. It cannot overrule the laws of nature outside of its own body. Don't be afraid of it. Soon Fr. Charles will be back. His prayers will drive it off."

The figure at the window continued to tap desperately at the door and window to create doubt as to who was the true mother. Then she eventually went off confused and worried and re-entered the church.

Inside the home, the imposter acted demurely and quietly when face to face with Elene but never allowed the outside Janice to see her face. She glanced at Elene out of the side of her eye.

"See, its gone. We have driven it off with spiritual music and faith. It's a thing of the lower regions, it cannot last long. It is an actor, a liar, an imitator and a returner from the grave."

Elene looked with fear at Blanche's body still hidden under the sheet.

She pondered, "I wonder?"

"Elene, why don't we look to make sure

that it really is Blanche under that shroud? Just to ease our minds."

"Yes, I agree," said Elene. "There is something here that is not as it should be. I feel it in the room and there's a strange smell too."

Slowly she approached the body of Blanche that still lay on a table.

"I must find out," she said.

She lifted the sheet, slowly pulled it back and looked. As she turned her back the false Janice silently began to assume a subtly threatening and sinister posture but changed to a demure and grateful and thankful posture as Elene turned towards her once more.

"It's her all right. Mother, I'm so glad. I was worried by a smell of strange spices and herbs in the air. I just wondered."

"Yes, I was worried too," said false Janice in a warm and friendly manner. "Just in case but it's all safe now that we know Blanche is not a returner."

Elene slowly replaced the shroud over Blanche. As she did so, the false mother still wearing Janice's clothes silently became the werewolf.

The werewolf howled and roared as she attacked Elene then threw her to the floor well away from the door. Elene screamed and attempted to fight back or run away but to no avail. She stumbled and fell.

Elene cried out in pain.

"Mother where are you? Where have you gone?"

Then she looked at the werewolf and screamed, "What are you? Where did you come from? Who are you? Why?"

Elene was soon overcome by the werewolf. During the final death throes she screamed and the werewolf's head and arms could clearly be seen at times. Then both became hidden behind the furniture. The werewolf roared and savaged its victim until at last there was a sudden silence as Elene perished.

However, there arose solemnly from the hidden death scene not the werewolf but Elene like a specter. The werewolf had now taken on her image.

False Elene's motions and gestures were a little more stiff than before. Her face was more grim and immobile but she gradually became more like the original without ever being quite as casual or emotional as before. There was a lingering stiffness in the imitation and an air of awkward hidden purpose.

The werewolf, now looking like Elene, took the shroud from the dead body of

Blanche and conspicuously threw it over the actual body of Elene.

The werewolf moved strangely towards the door, slightly awkward and ungainly as one trying to find its feet in new shoes. Then it opened the door.

"Mother where are you?" it called out. "Mother please don't hide. Where are you? I'm sorry I couldn't let you in earlier. My visitor was a parishioner speaking to me in confidence. I couldn't, just couldn't, let you in then. She begged me not to. Mother please come in."

False Elene stood sinisterly at the open door and beckoned with the left hand just as the werewolf had done previously when disguised as Michel and later when impersonating Fr. Charles in the church crypt. It was a slow, patient but somehow compelling gesture.

Then it spoke in a loud whisper.

"It's all right to come in now mother. The old lady has gone. It's all right mother. Please, what's the matter? Where are you?"

Janice was frightened, concerned and puzzled as she slowly came to the door.

"Are you all right, dear daughter?"

Then she touched Elene on the cheek, questioningly.

False Elene tried to reassure the

mother as she took her hand and smiled.

"Yes I'm fine. Of course I'm fine. I'm a little upset but come in."

Janice came in and false Elene closed the door with an air of satisfaction.

"Why would you not let me in earlier?" asked Janice. "I was so worried about you. I thought that all this trouble had upset your mind. Who was that woman you were so engrossed in speaking to? Where did she come from?"

False Elene pointed into the distance.

"She came in from the back door. She was just an old woman who wanted to get my advice. She asked me to keep her visit in confidence. That's why I couldn't let you in just at that moment."

Janice looked relieved but still puzzled as she touched the cheek of Elene again. Then she smiled and kissed her warmly.

False Elene positioned herself between Janice and the door and locked the multi-bolted door.

"Good, all is well then Elene," said the mother.

Janice suddenly noticed the body of Blanche uncovered and pointed to the sheet now covering a body on the floor.

"But what is that?"

She recoiled in horror.

False Elene responded in a mechanical attitude.

"It's the old lady. She died. I realized she was sick and dying that's why I could not let you in just then. It was her last hope for help. See, the dying need our help."

Janice was upset and worried again as she knelt down to remove the cover and look at the body. Suddenly she stood up in shock and confusion.

"It's you Elene. It's you lying dead and mutilated."

Then with terror in her voice, "I have gone insane. My mind is gone. This trouble has destroyed me."

Janice looked and pointed in horror at the body of Elene lying on the floor. As she did so the false Elene turned into the werewolf as before.

It laughed aloud as it grasped Janice by the throat.

"No, you're not insane, dear mother and you're not mad. You're just dead, dead, dead."

Janice was stunned as she sank down on her knees. She stared frozen with fear without any fight or flight and struggled little as the werewolf soon destroyed her life and threw her dead to the floor beside the body of her daughter Elene.

Once again there was the sound of tearing, devouring and savaging.

The werewolf, still dressed as false Elene, roared and growled as it unbolted the front door and rushed out. It laughed and laughed hysterically and screamed to the sky in victory. It howled to the moon and circled the house as it headed towards the graveyard.

It created mayhem in a frenzy of hatred as it ripped up bones and rocks, pushed over gravestones as before but more triumphantly as it threw out its arms in abandonment and worship to the moon. It roared and howled once more, then stopped, jumped and sniffed the air and snarled.

With its claws flexed, the werewolf looked around craftily and suspiciously as though suspecting a pursuer. Then it rushed off among the tombs and trees still laughing and howling to itself.

CHAPTER FIFTEEN

A Jury of Werewolves

A sudden thunderstorm beat against the windows of the abbey. The shadows of three empty nooses lit up by the flashes of lightning could be seen on the wall.

There was a long echoing knock on the door of the abbey. The two nuns, Sister Papillion and Prudence, opened the front door to Dr. Garzon and Felix O'Neill who had just returned from the graveyard. Both men were subdued and somber.

Inside the abbey it was moderately well lit as Sister Papillion ushered Felix O'Neill and Dr. Garzon into the library.

"Come in dear Mr. O'Neill and dear Dr. Garzon."

Prudence and Papillion bowed politely and at the same time they wrung their hands modestly.

"Please be comfortable," said Prudence. "Relax, sit down. The abbess is engaged but will be with you in a little while."

The sisters left the room and Dr. Garzon and Mr. O'Neill looked around uneasily and decided not to sit.

Then O'Neill spoke to Dr. Garzon in a soft whisper.

"I'm sure we were being followed through the graveyard and swamplands. Something was stalking us along the tombs and waterways to the abbey. Why did it not strike us? Does it know that I have a gun? And why is there a sickly smell of strange herbs in the air even here? Can this werewolf be everywhere or everyone?"

"You're right, O'Neill. Trudging here through the graveyard and the soggy paths and under the trees and bushes I expected something to strike but it did not. I don't know why. Indeed I don't even know what, much less who."

"I agree with you," said O'Neill. "It's time to point a finger but at whom? We can eliminate only the dead. A werewolf is a living person and not a creature of the supernatural."

"Well I'm not so sure about that," responded Garzon. "I still fear that magic may at least play a part somewhere."

Then Felix O'Neill's voice developed an accusing and scathing tone.

"Oh yes as with your second self, your astral projection. Remember?"

Garzon was astonished.

"Who me? Oh no, I meant someone else's second self."

"I mean it was your bright idea," said O'Neill slyly.

Garzon was flattered.

"Oh yes, of course old chap, astral projection, capital idea. And yes, through psychic magic."

"I call it secret science or super science," explained O'Neill.

"Perhaps," replied Garzon. "But then in that case the werewolf cannot be one of the local villagers. The werewolf can pass itself off as educated persons, therefore it must be sophisticated, familiar with polite society, at least by association. Of course the werewolf must be a master of super-science and it just might be cunning enough to conceal its true origins and pretend to be a yokel."

Then he looked around.

"Ugh, this place is eerie, strangely half-lit and shadowy."

"I can't argue with your logic," said O'Neill. "The killer could be an educated anyone."

"But if we're right," added Garzon, "that the werewolf is a clever and educated person, this limits the field of suspects to about a dozen."

"Yes, my dear Garzon," said O'Neill, "like the fleeting reverie of the suspects I had last night. A jury of twelve werewolves."

"What was that all about O'Neill?" asked a curious Dr. Garzon.

Then Felix O'Neill began to recall his strange reverie in some detail as an observer recounting scenes from his imagination.

"Let me tell you exactly what went through my mind last night as I thought about this climatic meeting," said Felix O'Neill.

"I was like a stranger observing the entire episode. It started with me watching you and I entering the abbey. You and I arrived at this abbey and entered into its dimly lit library. It was easy for me to imagine all twelve suspects congregating in the reading room and stating their cases one by one. In the mysterious atmosphere that pervaded the library I had imagined the testimony of the suspects one by one."

Twelve shadowy seats were ranged around in a circle. Felix O'Neill, dressed in outdoor clothing, began to sit quietly on one of the seats. He was tired and alone. He got up from the seat, yawned, and then sat down again. The lights faded where O'Neill was sitting and lit up the chairs around him. The other eleven chairs slowly filled up one by one with the shadowy suspects.

The last to arrive and take her place in the circle was Anne, the hostess of the inn.

Suddenly the voice of Felix O'Neill was heard to speak strangely and sleepily as in a trance.

"You the jury, whom do you find guilty?"

One by one the suspects stood up and confessed. The light faded on the others as one by one they all confessed their guilt. Each of the suspects stood in turn as Felix O'Neill seemed to hear dreamlike music invading the atmosphere.

Each confession was being imagined in the mind of Felix O'Neill. He was seeing a dramatized form of his thoughts about possible suspects.

The priest, Fr. Charles, was the first to stand up among the jurors.

"Yes, I am the werewolf. I truly report that I wish and I pray that I had not done what I did. I could not help it. This is an obscure and poor parish and I was sick of being poor and obscure. In my early days I was one of the top students in my seminary. If right had been done I would have received a parish in the rich farmland of the north but I had committed the great indiscretion of not ingratiating myself with the bishops and the archbishops and powerful church lawyers and politicians.

"I had always believed in humility and prayer and poverty and dependence on faith rather than churchmen. I believed in all the virtues but no, the true virtue is crawling to the powerful and to the wealthy patrons of the church. The true virtue is serving the selfish plans of the incompetent and lazy clerics."

He continued to speak with bitterness in his voice.

"Lacking the virtue of sycophancy I was sent to this desolate and penniless swampland parish.

"One night as I brooded bitterly, I had a change of mind, just that, a change of mind. I began to devote myself to research and to pursue the science of long life and power. Wealthy strangers are coming to my parish to study my secret formulas but they will never be able to prove anything against me because I now enjoy the protection of the most powerful. Yes, it was a small amount of deceit but it has brought me ambition renewed."

Fr. Charles finished speaking and then promptly sat down.

Pierre was the next to stand and make his confession.

"My body is weak and sick and my brothers and cousins were also weak and sick. They lived and died in poverty and never succeeded in life. Each day I feel troubled and unsettled in my mind but when I see something suffering it helps me just a little to feel good. I like to remind myself that I am not suffering as much as I might. Therefore I am superior to anything that is in greater pain. It calms my poor troubled mind to see something lying torn and bleeding and helpless. Peace enters my heart.

"To see some creature ripped apart is, to my mind, like a cool breath of ocean air to the congested lungs of the swamps. I need to breathe the clear sweet smell of blood in my lungs. Why should I not survive like everyone else? That is why I sought out wizards. That is why I have learned how to improve my weak body, my suffering body, into a strong wolfish tormentor. Why should fate have picked on me to be a weakling? Why me? What do I owe to those who are straight and strong?"

Then he laughed cynically.

"It's so good to rip them and tear them apart. It is life to me. To torment others is the true fulfillment of the surviving soul. Blood is my favorite sauce. Human is the meat I crave.*"*

He flexed his fingers then sat down again.

Anne, the hostess of the inn, was next to stand up.

"People despise me as a low-born peasant but as far as money goes I am the most successful person in the parish. I own the inn where travelers take their rest. The tavern where they eat and drink and are entertained, the livery stable, the horses that travelers buy and sell. The singers, the dancers in the tavern, all these I pay for and yet I am thought to be just a skivvy.

"I have long hoped for some kind of recognition or some little friendship or appreciation so I used my money to buy wisdom. The wisdom I sought and bought taught me that wealth does not lie in property but in the person. I learned how to invest in myself, in my person, not in my possessions.

"I acquired the strength and skills of the werewolf by dearly bought science. This made me strong in my body and well able to destroy some of those who shunned my friendship. All that I killed were subservient to the priest or to the canon or to the abbess. Even those whom I hired and fed ran to the masters or to the matriarch."

Her voice became stern.

"Mother or father I will not cringe to. I will try to focus the minds of our young people on their own trades and businesses and not to worship the old aristocracy with its courtesans. My killings will never be proven against me. For there is no personal hatred from me to them. No one will ever read my mind and prove this in a court of law."

Anne took her seat among the others.

Sergeant Antoine stood next.

"People laugh at me. I am considered to be a clown. I don't understand this. I do what I am told. I arrest whom I am told to arrest. If arrest means punishment and death for some, that is not my doing. Jail that man. I jail him. Yet they have mocked me and laughed at me, so I say: If I am a clown, then I am only the clown of law and order."

He stared ahead with contempt.

"I'm not supposed to have any feelings or opinions of my own. I'm sick of arresting dupes because I'm told to do so by all the greedy and grasping. I'm tired of letting the truly guilty go free because they are protected. I'm tired of being a tool of the rich against the poor. I begged and pleaded with those who have true wisdom and learnt the secret potions that made me as swift and self-satiating as a wolf. So I have been able to prey upon the liar, murder the fool and those who loved the tyrant and to destroy and tear apart the sons and daughters of privilege.

"When they meet me on a misty night, then they will not be given much to laughter, for then they will meet me as I really am. They expect me to arrest just anyone they tell me to. They expect me to be a crude and mindless machine but I'm not their dupe any more. Now I have my own ideas of whom I should arrest and why."

Sergeant Antoine took his seat and Doloree stood up next to confess.

"I admit it all. It was an evil thing to do, joining the coven of witches. They promised me protection, that if I joined then my superiors would protect me. I learnt that most of the wealthy have achieved their power through witchcraft. They persuaded me to become a witch so that I could seem to be in two places at one time. When I killed someone in one place, I would have witnesses that I was somewhere else at the time.

"In return for killing the people who were enemies of the coven, I was to be rewarded with health and friendship and respect. I know it was wrong to join the coven of witches but I was sick of being poor and going out on cold nights to bring healing into a world of poverty and misery. I just got so tired of the drudgery of it all, the aches and pains of old age and of poverty. Duplicity was my escape. I am weak now but I will be strong in the full moon. They think that they will kill me but they will see me rising up with the moon on a good night for werewolves and witches."

Doloree sat down among the others and Felix O'Neill took the witness stand to speak for himself.

"You may suspect that only I have the knowledge to deceive the masses. Ah, but think of the great knowledge of the dead. Can they come back to use their powerful science to tear apart and kill all whom they hate. Only I can explain these things or deceive you and throw you off my trail. These killings have nothing to do with advanced and forbidden secret-science as I suggested to mislead people.

"My true profession is that of a necromancer and from the beginning I have masterminded these killings from afar. The only power I have is, alas, over the dead and it is my mission to make the dead to walk and then to kill the living so as to bring about an equilibrium, an equality.

"In times past the living destroyed the dead. They called it cremation or burial or mummification but now the dead seek back their bodies and their resurrected life. Do not destroy them for the dead are my slaves, with them I play like any child with toys.

"What pleasure it gives me to send out my toy-things to scare and tear, jump out upon and tantalize their victims. Many and bored are the dead. What joy to give them strength to rise again and go to hide in forests and in houses and jump out upon the living. Boo, they say, ha, ha, boo, boo, I am the dead. I have an invitation for you to join me. Come to my region. Here, let me help you join me in the grave they plead with leaden eyes. And I say, Oh yes, I am the werewolf or rather the supervisor of the werewolves. The undead all, the zombies wearing the cloak of wolfery to confuse and put together a drama of playacting. What think you of the dead who walk at night?

"My toys are joined now by many more. Surely I have a right to be proud of them as they play their childish games of kill so well. The dead cry out in fun you are my long lost cousin, my next of kill, ha, ha. Run and see if you can lose me but ready or not here I kill. No longer bored now laughing are the dead."

Felix O'Neill laughed lightly as he sat down and Dr. Garzon now stood up to make his confession.

"No, you're all lying, I am the werewolf. It was my research into the magical mysteries that one day revealed the method to me. In ancient, forbidden, long hidden books I found the spells. The temptation was too great to feel the blood of youth once again charging through my veins. I thought I had covered my tracks too well to be discovered.

"To be academically bright is one thing and to pass exams telling what others have done, this is good and well in its place but it is a different thing entirely to get away with a massive deceit like this.

"First, I mastered the secret art of super-disguise then I visited these parts several times and many other places to gather the fluids of extended youth. I was afraid of being discovered when my friend, Mr. O'Neill, came here to investigate so I joined him to cover up my dangerous experiments. Still, my very knowledge of the occult made me an object of suspicion. I can only weep for the weak, broken bodies I have destroyed in my vain search for eternal youth through sorcery.

"The forbidden alchemy of turning a human into a superhuman chimera is something that must wait for the future and a more enlightened age. I was ahead of my time for today is the age of mere mortality. Tomorrow must come the day of eternal youth. However, I hope that I have made some small contribution towards the wonders of tomorrow."

With that triumphant call to arms for future science, Dr. Garzon took his seat among the others.

The abbess was next to stand proudly in the witness stand.

"Of course I am Zakotu the werewolf. I am the descendent of the ancient tribe of Zakotu who once ruled all of these waterlands and islands before the thefts and ravages of newcomers. I am a true native of these mysterious regions.

"I determined to join a traditional order of nuns who have long lived among these peoples and these coasts and so to extend my power over them as long as possible. So I used the ancient sorcery of the tribe of Zakotu that had come down to me as an inheritance to give me the strength and endurance, then I improved with knowledge from all ages and sciences the secret of super-strength and extended life.

"I towered in power and mind-strength over these poor fishing people. Indeed, I tore out their throats and devoured their blood to establish my ascendancy over them and theirs. Soon all these swamps will be mine just as my ancestors ruled in total power over the ancient fisher-folk and the strange creatures of these waters and rivers.

"To make them suspicious of each other, to fear each other, to divide, to play with and to manipulate. All this is my destiny, to rule and to reign and to subjugate the lesser people and to live a long good life. This is the reward of wisdom. This is my birthright as a true descendent of the Zakotu clan. Yes, I am Zakotu the werewolf."

When the Abbess Concordee sat down, the sisters Papillion and Prudence stood up together and spoke one at a time.

Prudence was first to speak.

"We have had hatred and suspicion heaped upon us because of the old torture machinery which still lies unused in our abbey. But we have surpassed the old machinery with our ability to tear apart evildoers as we took the form of wolves."

Then Papillion spoke on her own.

"All we ever wanted was to discover the truth."

Prudence interrupted.

"Yes, so that evildoers can be punished and prevented."

Papillion spoke up.

"People condemn us for working in the old abbey museum of truth. But we are servants of a very fine lady. Her highness the Mother Superior has a duty to help keep law and order so that her religious and other dependents can live in freedom from burnings and lootings and disruptions of orderly life. Let all things be done decently and in order."

Prudence added.

"If you ask a criminal if he did wrong and he says, No, I'm a good man, no definitely not, do you say thank you sir, you may go? Sorry I troubled you. Do you take his word for it? You may say look at evidence. But suppose that the evidence is hidden, not there, then do you take his word for it? Ah yes, is he innocent because he says he is innocent?"

Papillion flexed her claws viciously.

"Or do you inquire more deeply into the truth by means of a few tricks and the sight of simple machine aids to memory and honesty? Why, according to some, were those old inquisitors so bad? They looked only for truth."

Prudence asked.

"Do you let the assassin walk free on his own word or do you inquire more thoroughly? It has been such a grief to us that the greatest malefactors could not be put to the test here by our truth machines. They could not be arrested because they were powerful or enjoyed the protection of some wealthy one, so they were free to cheat and steal."

Papillion commented.

"Still, the abbess is a lady of very high standards. She wishes only the best, peace and tranquility for her religious sisters and the parishioners. She needs help to keep most people honest and decent.

"Our machinery is excellent but we are not permitted to use it any longer. It has been proscribed by the church and banned for hundreds of years. Now it just so happens that some of our neighbors were bad. Yes, bad neighbors filled with spite and jealousy because of our position of trust with the abbess. You do need to deal with bad neighbors you know.

"So my dear sister and I sought out a wise witch who tutored us in the art of shapeshifting and we, with potions and strange devices, were able to acquire the strength of wolves which we, as weakly women, did not normally have. Thus we could use the strength of wolves to strike a blow for justice and for truth."

Then Prudence added.

"Yes, serving in a different way the same purpose as our old outdated inquisitional machinery to separate the truthtellers from the liars. By stalking the truth-destroyers and scandalmongers and destroying them."

Papillion added.

"We too have alternated in disguise, each providing an alibi for the other. Witchery learned from the books of the great library showed us the way. We are the werewolves. We are justified. All of those who died were evildoers."

Prudence pointed out.

"We crawl and creep out in the dark by the eternal principle of death to all the wrongdoers. Slaughter us if you will for our good conscience but we will kill the evil ones of the swamplands."

Then the two sisters finished their confessions and sat down together.

Canon Louis twitched as he stood up in some anguish.

"I confess I am the werewolf. It has nothing to do with magic or spells or secret-science or trying to find the fountain of eternal youth or serving vigilante-type justice. No, none of the things so foolishly dreamed up. No, it was just a simple matter of my being born. I was born with that rare but fatal genetic disorder "lycanthropy" or "wolfism".

He twitched insidiously.

"All humans are related to primates and so all humans are related indirectly to all creatures. Sometimes genetic patterns lose their way, throwbacks we know of but there are also cross throwbacks. These are rare occurrences of genetic mis-planting such as goat-people like Pan, horse-humans or centaurs or birdmen. I was born a half-wolf under the skin. Wolf-creatures are just mistakes of nature. I could not help it."

He raised his hands and twitched.

"This is a great advantage to me. I am stronger and faster than the merely normal. Why should I not kill those born to be my inferior? This is the eternal law of evolution.

"What right had nature to make me a freak? What do I owe to the world except revenge? What do I owe to fate except my extra strength and the resentment of an outcast?"

Canon Louis sneered at the others as he sat down again.

Professor Vermillion slowly stood up to speak and occasionally removed her glasses, polished them and replaced them.

"I am the nurse in the night. I am the elusive visitor of White Chapel - the lady with the little black bag. I am the stranger who comes by and whom people scarcely notice. The casual stranger who fits into the background. Yes, I am the werewolf. None of you guessed because of my acting but now it is too late. For the abbess and canon and priest must find other suspects guilty because some of those fools have confessed. And to release suspects now would cause a riot - a revolution that would overthrow the local powerlords.

"My disguise as an impartial co-investigator was the perfect way to find out who knew what and those who knew or suspected I soon disposed of. Yes, I am a scholar of the ancient sciences of shape-shifting. I have long been among you in one form or another. I was the traveler who just happened to come by when the boyfriend of the kitchenmaid was killed. I impersonated her boyfriend after I had killed him. I am the perennial stranger. I am the merciful visiting nurse, the lady with the lamp. I am the shadowy one who lingers innocently in woods and coaches and in dark corners.

"I am the stranded traveler who walks the railway station late at night or early in the morning. I am the casual observer who appears at the street corner after a late night revel. Quietly I watch the partygoers go their ways. Then I follow one of them.

"I am the officer of the law who walks a lonely beat in the evening, eager to help the straggler on his way. I am also everyman or sometimes everywoman who unexpectedly appears as a companion in the dusk. People go missing and are never seen again. Usually I bury the bodies in the graveyard but sometimes I get careless, perhaps even arrogant and I leave the bodies unburied. This gives me pleasure to see the same fear and torment on the faces of the living as on the dead.

"Beware of the unknown visitor who happens by. She too may be a werewolf. Or he, looking out of the side of his eye, Pardon me sir, could you help my little sick dog? Could you help me with this box, my leg is lame or could you direct me? Later the tale is told, He or she disappeared - apparently left home without a message, ran off with someone, gone forever. Beware of the opportune, the kindly, helpful lady or the gentleman who helps out in the dusk. Yes, I am the nurse of the night."

Professor Vermillion bowed and sat down among the other juror-suspects in the shadows of the old library.

Felix O'Neill remained calm, thoughtful and contemplative as the light slowly began to fade in the library and he imagined that he could hear the sound of faint dream-like music in the distance.

"Well, that was the entire daydream, the complete reverie, Garzon," said Felix O'Neill. "Make what you like of it."

"Absolutely astounding my dear chap," said Dr. Garzon as he shook his head in amazement.

CHAPTER SIXTEEN
The Werewolf Identified

Felix O'Neill and Dr. Garzon were still in the library discussing the strange reverie when the abbess came into the room. She was cheerful.

"I couldn't help overhearing some of that speculation. What a strange work of fiction you two seem to have concocted between you."

Felix O'Neill was apologetic.

"As you noted Abbess we were just speculating who might be the murderer."

The abbess was slightly displeased and cold in her reply.

"Dr. Garzon you are not only a very well qualified healtharian but Mr. O'Neill has the imagination of a true writer. Yes indeed, some very dubious characters describe themselves as creative artists but both of you really do have very vivid imaginations and the potential of becoming great writers."

Dr. Garzon was oblivious of the implied criticism and replied with great pride.

"Oh thank you, ma'am. You're so kind to say so."

The abbess interrupted him and turned away to address Felix O'Neill in a sharper tone.

"Mr. O'Neill, although you are no doubt a true scholar of the occult, you are not in touch with real people. But rather you are somewhere up in the clouds flying among the wizards and witches."

At this comment Felix O'Neill cut in.

"Obviously you've been listening to our speculations for some time Abbess and you seem to have overheard every word we said. And for some reason you are upset and annoyed with our efforts."

Then he turned away and put his hands in his pockets.

"After all we were merely trying to identify the werewolf, the shapeshifter."

Dr. Garzon looked at O'Neill and nodded attentively.

As both their backs were partly turned, the abbess began to become wolfish and flexed her hands like claws.

Suddenly O'Neill turned around with a large revolver in his hand and caught the abbess unawares in her wolfish posture.

"So it was you?" said Felix O'Neill. "You are the werewolf, Abbess."

Then he shot her full in the chest. The abbess, mortally wounded, fell against a bookcase as blood poured from her chest. As she sank to her knees, she looked stunned at the blood that was draining through her fingers as though unbelieving of what she saw.

The abbess now became weak and drained of life and hope.

"Oh Mr. O'Neill, all the research, all the science and all the hope that I had to stay alive, you have killed it all. All my scientific experiments gone and lost to humanity forever."

"Maybe," replied O'Neill, "but you have lied and killed my friends. Friends do mean something to me, like Sergeant Antoine and Madame Vermillion. Where are they?"

"They are quite safe Mr. O'Neill, merely being held for questioning with Sister Doloree inside the old abbey."

Then she pointed breathlessly.

Felix O'Neill became saddened as he considered the loss to science for a moment.

"I am sorry Abbess Concordee. What you say might have been quite possible except for one thing, that day you killed Blanche my protégée the one I said I would protect and help. That day I promised myself that I would kill you, whoever you were and so I did and so you are the dead werewolf."

Dr. Garzon looked dubious and fearful.

"My dear O'Neill, are you quite sure the abbess was the werewolf?"

CHAPTER SEVENTEEN

Judgment and Mystery

The sound of the shot had echoed in the abbey. Suddenly Canon Louis came running into the library along with Pierre and the sisters, Prudence and Papillion.

Canon Louis cried out, "Abbess is everything O.K.? We heard a shot."

Then seeing the abbess lying on the floor and Felix O'Neill with a smoking gun in his hand, they all stepped back in fear. When Canon Louis realized that Mr. O'Neill was not threatening them, he advanced towards Felix and Dr. Garzon.

He called out for the guards.

"Guards, guards, come here quickly. Hand over your gun Mr. O'Neill. You can't kill us all. The abbey is alive with soldiers. Your gun please."

The canon twitched violently.

Felix O'Neill handed over his gun. Then Pierre, Canon Louis and the sisters surrounded O'Neill and Dr. Garzon.

Canon Louis retained Felix O'Neill's gun and pointed it at the two suspects.

Pierre drew his sword.

The sisters, Prudence and Papillion, pointed their fingers shakily at the two suspects.

Felix O'Neill and Dr. Garzon were then backed against a wall and handcuffed by a guard.

Canon Louis went to attend to the abbess and decided to get a doctor for her.

"Mother of the abbey you are badly hurt."

He looked inquiringly at the abbess.

"No, I was shot and well shot with a good bullet," insisted the abbess. "Let me die."

The abbess gasped and then continued breathlessly.

"It was just as I feared. I had a dream so alive and so often that warned me it would be so. I would one day be shot. But how or when it would happen I did not know. So I was wary of guns. But to no avail. This was my destiny."

She held her chest as she tried to continue breathing.

"Fiends," rasped Pierre. "So you are murderers come to kill Mother Concordee. Mother of all these islands and waterways and her devoted religious ones."

Prudence was horrified.

"Felix O'Neill, are you the killer or is it your assistant or both of you? How can you kill one so good and kind as the abbess? How can you kill a wise and goodly mother? Are you both grim werewolves?"

Sisters Papillion and Prudence began to chatter to themselves in fear, almost half-wittedly.

"We are not werewolves," insisted Dr. Garzon. "Since when does a werewolf shoot with a gun? If we were werewolves we could break these handcuffs and roar and tear apart all who oppose us. We're just a healer and a detective who seek only the truth. We harm no one."

"Good liars," said Papillion. "Isn't that what werewolfism is all about? Soon we'll have you in our own confessional. Not a trap hole where priests squint through the window. But a large and airy and pleasant chamber equipped with all traditional and modern aids to get true confessions."

Canon Louis admonished the sisters and Pierre.

"What you are threatening is forbidden madness. No one may torture anyone. Go and fetch the priest. He is on his way to the abbey and bring more guards here. Where are they? Are they all sleeping?"

Pierre departed.

The abbess was dying and sank low.

"No. No. I wish no rites, no priest, no ceremonies. My servants Pierre and my two dearest sisters have done no harm to anyone."

She continued to gasp for air.

"They did not understand what they were doing. I ordered them to do this or that or I would have put them out to die in the world. They truly love the swampland people."

The abbess held her chest and gasped once more.

Canon Louis twitched again, No, No. Then he pointed to Felix O'Neill and Dr. Garzon.

"Of course," agreed the canon, "No blame attaches to Pierre and the two sisters. Rather, these two are the perpetrators of this malice."

The abbess became menacing as she looked at Felix O'Neill.

"Mr. O'Neill, I would like to talk to you about the science."

"Why?" said Felix O'Neill. "I have nothing to say to you Abbess and you no more to say to me. Only the strike of death can pierce your heart. Pleas and tears and prayers meant nothing to you as you killed not a few but more and more pale victims in your thirst for life."

Canon Louis and the two religious sisters recoiled in fear at these words of Mr. O'Neill and in terror of the imminent demise of the abbess.

Canon Louis twitched wildly, No, No.

"Surely you are not accusing Abbess Concordee of these werewolf crimes, Mr. O'Neill?"

"Why else is she exonerating her servants, unless she is the werewolf?" asked Felix O'Neill. "Why would I shoot her? She is the deceiver and the shapeshifter. The thief prolonging her life by devouring other lives. The one who stalks the woods at night. The actor who enters into our homes and mocks and laughs. A deathly comedian and a cunning practitioner of the secret science of life. Search for all the papers of her sad experiments and see for yourself."

"Silence," demanded Canon Louis. "Your words are poison, you scandalous charlatan. I charge you both with murder. Also you are charged with blasphemy and insurrection, with witchcraft and turning yourselves into sly werewolves."

Pierre returned with Fr. Charles and two soldiers. The guards took over from the sisters the task of guarding Dr. Garzon and Felix O'Neill who were still handcuffed and standing against the wall.

The priest hurried to the side of the dying abbess. But unseen to the others she had already turned into a werewolf as she lay dying in the shadows.

The priest knelt beside her and then drew back in horror as he raised his voice.

"This is not Abbess Concordee. This is the werewolf wearing the clothes of the abbess. I cannot give the rites of final healing to a creature from the pit. This is beyond humanity."

Pierre and the canon approached the body of the abbess and lights were brought over to establish that she was indeed now a werewolf.

They were all horrified at the sight of the dead werewolf which was bleeding and red in the chest where it had been shot in the heart.

Fr. Charles looked around.

"Why are Dr. Garzon and Mr. O'Neill being held captive here?"

Canon Louis became uncertain and twitched nervously.

"They shot the abbess. As you see, she is now dead."

Then he placed the back of his hand across his mouth in confusion.

"But this is the werewolf," exclaimed

Fr. Charles. "Look, see for yourself. If this is the abbess she has turned into a wolf. It is no crime to kill a killer wolf. Release these investigators immediately. They have been trying to help us."

Canon Louis hesitated and examined the body of the abbess. He was confused but reluctantly concurred with the priest. He nodded solemnly then twitched, No, No.

"Yes, true indeed, the abbess has turned into a werewolf as you said."

Then he spoke to the guards.

"Release these prisoners and release any others held in the museum. They too are clearly victims of the werewolf."

The guards released Dr. Garzon and Felix O'Neill and then departed towards the presumed museum.

Pierre and the two sisters looked at first confused and then disgusted. Then they slunk slowly towards the front door of the abbey as they headed out towards the museum.

"You fool," said Pierre. "Canon Louis don't you realize that you and all of us who served the Mother Concordee will now be convicted as aiders and abetters of the werewolf. Soon you'll be in jail and then us. We will all swing. You are an imbecile. Spoiler of natural justice."

The sisters hid guiltily behind Pierre.

Canon Louis twitched, No. No.

"I try for justice. I may not be a genius but justice I do try to serve. And you are right about one thing, as close collaborators of the werewolf you three are suspect despite the Mother's last pathetic attempt to exonerate you all. You must have suspected that she was the werewolf. Guards, guards, where are you? Come quickly and arrest these collaborators?"

Pierre drew two knives from his belt and threw them at Fr. Charles and Canon Louis. The priest was hit only slightly in the arm but Canon Louis was struck in the chest and died almost instantly.

Then the two old sisters and Pierre hurried away from the abbey while Fr. Charles knelt briefly beside Canon Louis.

The priest shook his head in sorrow, prayed briefly then rose to his feet.

"Those killers won't get very far. Word travels like a bird among the fishing folk of the waterways. Somehow news seems to travel faster than you or I can ride or sail a boat."

"Why not?" agreed Mr. O'Neill. "A voice can carry well over a watery swamp or across a tangled marshland where never a horse can ride."

"Yes indeed, Mr. O'Neill. The whole village and neighborhood will soon be out looking for them. Even now the local people may be talking about the killing of Mother Concordee and are beginning to come out of their homes to celebrate the death of the unknown one they called by tradition - Zakotu the werewolf."

Then an atmosphere of quietness fell upon the room as Mr. O'Neill went and stood over the body of the werewolf.

The guards returned with Professor Vermillion, Doloree and Sergeant Antoine. As they entered the room, they looked at the Mother Superior stretched out as a wolf in her nun's clothing.

Felix O'Neill turned towards the others and addressed Madame Vermillion.

"So Madame you were arrested and dragged into the depths of this abbey?"

Then Dr. Garzon stretched his hands towards the professor.

"Are you all right? Are you unharmed Madame? Can I get you an escort to the tavern?"

Professor Vermillion trembled in terror and confusion.

"No I'm fine Dr. Garzon, thank you. Now that I see the werewolf is dead I feel much better. And so the Abbess Concordee was the werewolf and you killed her Dr. Garzon, just as you said you would? Well done."

Garzon pointed at O'Neill.

"I'm afraid I can't take the credit for that Madame. It was Mr. O'Neill who killed the werewolf."

O'Neill shook his head just a little sadly as if to say that killing was no pleasure to him.

Professor Vermillion looked at him in confusion.

"Really, Mr. O'Neill?"

"Yes Professor, I realized that someone in authority must have had you all arrested or removed to somewhere for the purpose of keeping everything quiet."

As they were talking, Fr. Charles called out to the sergeant and the guards.

"Why are you waiting here? Get out. Arrest Pierre and Prudence and Papillion, the collaborators of the Abbess Concordee, the werewolf."

"Indeed Fr. Charles with the greatest pleasure," said Sergeant Antoine. "But first let me explain how we were taken. We were captured by Pierre and two guards and taken to the torture chamber. Madame Vermillion and I were imprisoned alongside Doloree by Pierre and the two mad sisters.

It was clear that the abbey was the center of the werewolf's prowlings, so we would never have been allowed to live to tell the tale. They were just beginning to torture us to make us confess. It was getting unpleasant until your people rescued us just in time."

Then Sergeant Antoine and the guards saluted the others as they all marched towards the front door in obedience to Fr. Charles' orders.

"Let me join you Sergeant Antoine," said Professor Vermillion as she adjusted her glasses and squinted. "You may need a witness to speak to the crowd and testify about the werewolf, in order to calm the chaos. I may be of help."

"Sure, come with us Professor, this will be your chance to give some real help to the people."

Then Sergeant Antoine addressed Fr. Charles.

"Thank you Fr. Charles for this great opportunity, your reverence. Those orders are the sweetest I have ever received. This is now my chance to raise up the commonwealth."

Then the sergeant departed, shouting orders to the guards.

"Come fools. Now is your chance to make amends and correct all your old mistakes. If you can capture these three perhaps I will forgive you for arresting us. I may even reinstate you."

The guards looked guilty and confused.

Dr. Garzon, Felix O'Neill and Doloree stood together and looked down at the werewolf, the Abbess Concordee, the dead Mother Superior. Then Dr. Garzon put his arm around Doloree.

"You are safe now, dear lady."

"I thank you all for helping me," said Doloree. "I am only a poor old woman, a nobody."

"Doloree you are the survivor of a great injustice," said Felix O'Neill. "You are only one of many whom we tried to save because so many people like you have had lives destroyed by the werewolf."

Then he pointed towards the werewolf.

"Yes, it was a great waste of genius. And there she lies, as those who hounded her will one day lie, so still and small and broken like those she killed. The things she dreaded most have now come true. She lies alone and cold and locked in her own mind. She is not able to break through those window eyes, not seeing all the things around her. Frozen, victor and victim will both lie the same. And so the abbess has gone her own lonely and strange way."

The others nodded sadly as Mr. O'Neill continued.

"The Abbess Concordee killed too often and too coldly to support her own strange experiment with life. It was all wrong but it is all so sad - a science gone astray."

As the lights grew dim in the library, slowly the group departed through the front door of the abbey.

Fr. Charles walked alongside Doloree, followed by Dr. Garzon and lastly Mr. Felix O'Neill.

CHAPTER EIGHTEEN
The Departures

Now that the werewolf was no longer able to terrorize the inhabitants of the village, there was now no trace of the sinister and mysterious atmosphere that pervaded the streets outside the village inn.

There was no doubt that anyone was whom they appeared to be and all speech was frank and without hidden connotations. There was just a hint of sadness for the recent killings and just a touch of nostalgia because of departed friends.

The time had now come for Dr. Garzon and Felix O'Neill to leave for the long journey back to their homes. Soon they both appeared dressed for travel with cloaks and hats and carrying valises. They put down their baggage and Dr. Garzon sat while Felix O'Neill paced up and down as they waited for their coach to arrive.

Dr. Garzon looked at his watch and suggested that they wait for the professor.

"Let's wait here for Madame Vermillion before we join the coach. She'll be here shortly."

O'Neill nodded but was a little preoccupied as he continued to walk up and down.

"There's still trouble going on here you know. Since the two senior nuns and the curator were captured and found guilty of aiding and abetting the werewolf there have been signs of some civil unrest."

Garzon agreed.

"Unrest? No one will rest until all the guilty have been dealt with, executed or banished or sentenced to life - whatever."

"I suppose it's none of our business Garzon now we've done our part," remarked O'Neill.

Soon Professor Vermillion arrived also dressed for travel.

"I'm still not sure how you figured it out Mr. O'Neill," she queried.

"Everything depended on my basic premise which was that the super-science of rejuvenation and shapeshifting was the key, Professor. This secret-science required a person with education and intelligence and there are only a few such people in the vicinity. I would say there's about a dozen or so educated people living here. A strong smell of garlic and herbs was in her abbey that night.

"A werewolf from the outside was unlikely to have invaded the abbey since it's built like a fortress to protect the nuns. The swish of skirts was there, as heard by many victims.

"Then a stronger clue was the fact that the abbess read many books by early Christian writers who dealt specifically with werewolfism and sorcery. Sorcery, I believe to be an early form of secret-science."

"Which writers my dear O'Neill?" inquired Dr. Garzon. "Evidently your Irish Roman Catholic background has served you well in this matter."

"Well for instance, there was St. John Chrysostom and St. Augustine who have both written outstandingly on delusion and secret-science and shapeshifting."

"Hmm, I noticed books by both of those authors on her table in the library," remarked the professor, "but I didn't know that they wrote a lot about such things."

"Yes, that was my first clue," said O'Neill. "And also in our final confrontation with the abbess I turned suddenly to catch a glimpse of her getting ready to strike us from behind."

Dr. Garzon shook his head.

"So you shot her. I admit that I was scared to death when you did that. I have always looked on shapeshifting, not as true science but sorcery of the night."

"So what is the real difference?" asked O'Neill.

"My view is that sorcery involves moral reprobation," replied Dr. Garzon, "evil is involved not just science but science forbidden."

"My dear Mr. O'Neill," said Professor Vermillion, "this revives the question, What is shapeshifting? What kind of secret-science or magic is it? What are the formulas, the herbs, drugs or chemicals that cause the delusions? How does the sorcerer or the scientist seize the power of animalistic strength and rejuvenation - blood, glands, brain serum, genes - how?"

"The fires and looting by the local fishing people have destroyed or stolen all traces of the Abbess Concordee's notes and lab equipment," said O'Neill.

"We'll never know now exactly. But remember that I told you about my dream of a werewolf trial where I went through the roll-call of all the suspects. Then I came to realize that the abbess was eavesdropping on my conversation about her guilt. My version of her possible confession seemed to unsettle and unbridle her. So it must have come pretty close to the mark."

"But if we don't know exactly how shapeshifters work, how can we find them or tell how many other werewolves there are in the world?" asked Professor Vermillion.

Felix O'Neill agreed.

"All apparently good citizens, friends of the community."

"But wolves in sheep's clothing," said Dr. Garzon.

O'Neill paused for thought.

"Yes and so Abbess Concordee's secret-science died with her. She was a deceiver and liar and cunning impersonator. Yet strangely she had a terrible integrity like an olden queen of secret astrological numbers. She was a mistress of illusion and disguise and a manipulator of mindmadness and fear. What lonely sciences perished when she died?"

"I hope and pray that the dark powers will never permit her to come back. May she rest in peace," said Dr. Garzon.

Then Garzon became sad.

"Indeed, let only those judge her who understand the torment of the soul sinking into darkness."

At this point in the conversation, Fr. Charles, Doloree, the sergeant and Anne all joined the company.

Sergeant Antoine pointed towards the distance and shook his head.

"The coach is here to take you to the steamboat. Ah, that you should leave us all so soon."

He took the bags belonging to Mr. O'Neill and Dr. Garzon and moved them.

"Everyone has come to bid you all farewell," he said.

"But we invite you back soon, very soon," said Anne the hostess of the inn. "All the village and fishing people will welcome you, now that the old abbey is closed and the nuns have been dispersed. Before you three came it was a stormy night but now you are leaving on a bright morning."

Then she kissed Madame Vermillion on the cheek and shook hands with Dr. Garzon and Felix O'Neill.

"Thank you," said O'Neill. "And again, congratulations Ann on your engagement to Sergeant Antoine."

Antoine and Anne were pleased to acknowledge the compliment.

"And congratulations Doloree on your new job as housekeeper to Fr. Charles."

"I thank you all," said Doloree.

"You'll be kept busy Doloree," said Fr. Charles. "It's a big presbytery but it's better than walking the roads at all hours."

"And some work for you here too, Fr. Charles," remarked Dr. Garzon, as he looked towards Anne and Sergeant Antoine. "I'm very surprised that a free-thinker like Sergeant Antoine wants to actually get married."

Sergeant Antoine looked at Anne.

"She is so beautiful, I just can't help it. Please forgive me."

Then he changed the tone in his voice to sound more accusing.

"It's all your fault Anne. If only you were ugly I could resist you. To think that the Abbess Concordee killed so many good people and so many wicked wretches like my mother still live. It's an unjust world. It only goes to prove, Father, that there is no such thing as the hand of providence. The hand of providence is withered or at best paralyzed. You must admit it's true, Father."

"You shock us all terribly, Sergeant," said Fr. Charles sounding kind and casual.

Sergeant Antoine was pleased and grinned from ear to ear as he grabbed the bags belonging to the three travelers.

"Thank you, Fr. Charles. I do my best. I'll leave quickly while it is still safe. I think I hear my mother coming."

"My dear O'Neill," said Dr. Garzon, "before we leave can you now reveal the name of the person who invited you here."

"Certainly, my dear Garzon."

"Then who was it, O'Neill?"

"I have just told you. Garzon."

"Who? Garzon? Who is that? Oh, you don't mean me, old chap?"

He laughed loudly.

"Yes, I remember saying that you should look into that werewolf business. And so you did my dear O'Neill, very well indeed."

Suddenly the sound of mob rioting was heard and the window of the old museum chamber lit up where the three empty hangman's nooses had always been seen. The window appeared in the light of a red fire that showed the silhouette of Pierre which hung from the middle noose and the two sisters swinging on either side. Red flames illuminated the shadowy silhouettes as the background noise of mob rioting continued.

"Since you brought about the whole adventure Garzon, I'll permit you the last word on the werewolf."

"Thank you, Felix. I would only add, here you see Zakotu the werewolf pass into history and peace return to the villages of the great swamplands.

"However, there are some who may disagree. There are some who will say that elsewhere in the world, when sleet knocks on the window - tap, tap, tap - and when the night is chilly and damp on the spine – then beware.

"When furious raindrops like cold fingers try the handles and press against the rattling quaking doors of the home – then beware again.

"When there is a wind insistently whispering - let me in - let me in - then beware of the casual stranger who comes by. For then, it may be that the abbess as a Vampire will walk again.

"So beware. That is what some would say and indeed, who can tell?"

Felix O'Neill and Dr. Garzon shook hands in a congratulatory mood.

Then Dr. Garzon, Felix O'Neill and Professor Vermillion walked together to the awaiting coach.

Doloree, Fr. Charles, Sergeant Antoine and Anne waved at the coach and four as it departed. Shouts of goodbye and waves came from the three travelers as the others slowly returned to their homes.

Meanwhile in the graveyard there was the sound of a furious storm stirring. Wind, rain and thunder as flashes of lightning lit up the gravestones.

Slowly the image of Abbess Concordee rose up from among the graves - an apparition that continued to brood over the entire swampland.

The End

Beware of the Casual Stranger

www.ingramcontent.com/pod-product-compliance
Lightning Source LLC
Chambersburg PA
CBHW070830120626
46556CB00002B/696